FINDING DIRECTION

WITH THE BAND

BOOK ONE

TANYA RENEE

Serenade
Publishing

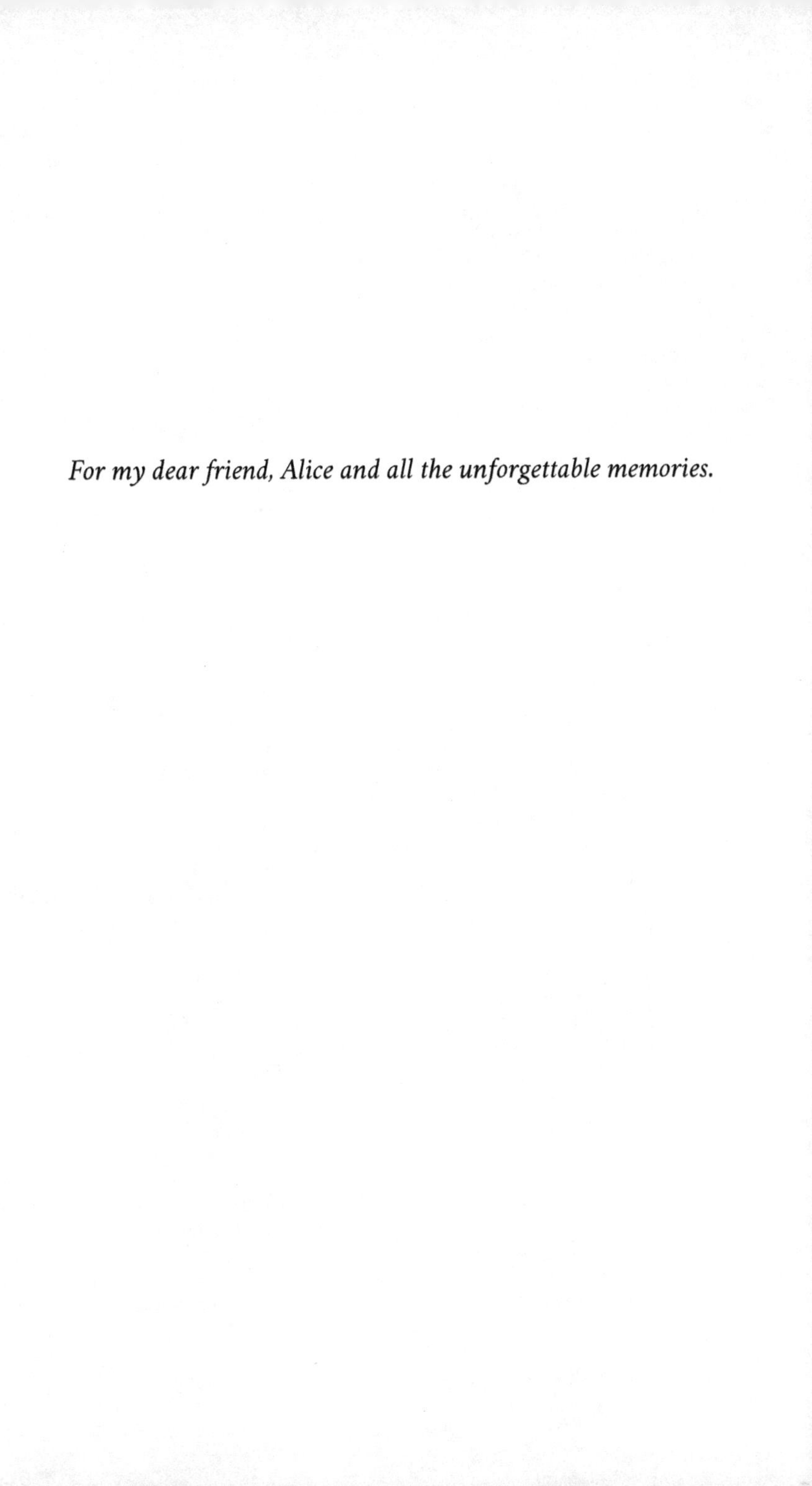

For my dear friend, Alice and all the unforgettable memories.

ALSO BY TANYA RENEE

Primrose Series

Prairie Sky

Prairie Nights

Prairie Fire

Prairie Hearts

Prairie Sound

With The Band

Finding Direction

Love Notes

PROLOGUE

PRESENT DAY

Late summer brought an inevitable chill to the air, promising fall around the corner. Layne Stark sat on his deck sipping a cup of coffee, watching the steam curl above his mug as he reflected on this past summer. The fun of performing with his best friends and bandmates. The thrill of seeing their songs charting and hearing their music on the radio. Witnessing his dearest friend, Rami getting engaged to the love of his life. Layne breathed deeply, the crisp air filling his lungs and numbing his heart as memories floated into his consciousness.

Every year, the back-to-school season brought him back eight years ago, to a day he would never forget. A day so burned into his memory that it was now ingrained in his soul. The overwhelming pangs of loneliness set in as they always did at this time of year. Loneliness that he caused and could never overcome despite every attempt at trying. Layne was sure it was unhealthy to still feel this way. Still holding onto the past and bringing himself through the process of self-loathing that always seemed to accompany the memories. A lifetime worth of memories of an unforgettable year. Memories that were etched into the fabric of who he was and that made his heart ache with excruciating pain every time he thought about her.

Juli. A girl with beautiful doe-like brown eyes that he was certain could see into his soul. A girl with a smile brighter than the sun, that instantly captured his heart the first time she offered it to him. A smile that was sweet, honest, and pure. A smile that was washed away the last time they saw each other. Melted away by a flood of tears.

Regret. It is a nasty emotion. An emotion that eats away at you daily, especially when that regret involves someone you love with your entire heart and soul. Someone you still love today, despite time and distance. Someone whose face you still see when you close your eyes at night.

Layne closed his eyes and took a deep breath, letting it out slowly in a long exhale, trying to tamp down the emotions those memories brought on. He set his coffee cup down, reached for his phone, and swiped it open. He clicked on a text from Rami.

Rami: Are you ready to take Europe by storm? 25 dates in 2 1/2 months.

Layne: As ready as I'll ever be. Are you okay leaving Savanah and your newly engaged world for that long?

Rami: We're in a good place. I'll miss her terribly, but it will make the homecoming that much sweeter.

Layne smiled. His best friend was deeply in love and although they had a few obstacles along the way, they ultimately found their way back to each other. Sighing, he put down his phone and closed his eyes, trying to wrestle the memories away as he let the cool of the morning breeze wash over him. He was in love once and she loved him. That was until he pushed her away and broke her tender heart. *You were so stupid. So young and so incredibly scared and stupid.* He shook his head, attempting to silence that self-loathing voice again. *You need to stop, Layne.*

Glancing at his phone again, he pulled up the schedule for the tour and his eyes immediately zoned in on Hamburg, Germany. One show, three full days in the city. The city that Juli called home.

Finding her on social media years ago, he was too scared to friend her, opting to secretly watch her life unfold over the past eight years. As he scrolled through her feed, he was always filled with a deep longing and hope that one day their paths would cross again. That fate would forgive his past transgressions and somehow, someway, she might forgive him too. This tour was his opportunity to do just that. To right the wrongs that he caused, no matter what the outcome. *Would she be at the show? Would she want to see me again? Or am I just a past memory? A bad memory of the boy that shattered her heart.*

CHAPTER 1

PRESENT DAY

Tucking the newspaper under her arm, Juliana Roth strolled down the stone patchwork quilt street in the HafenCity Hamburg business district. This waterfront development with its tall redbrick buildings, dappled with interesting modern architecture, was the epitome of chic with its old meets new vibe. She crossed a promenade, her heeled boots making that satisfying tapping sound on the stone as she glanced down at a tour boat on the Elbe River full of tourists, many of which offering her a friendly wave. Obliging with a smile, she waved back as she straightened out her thick wool scarf around her neck. It was getting colder and the chill of the morning wind off the water bit at her skin, making it tingle and burn from the cold. Reaching the publishing house, she slipped inside the door to be met by a blast of warmth and sighed in relief. Giving the security guard a little wave with her mittened hand, she sprinted to the elevator before the door closed and shimmied herself inside the already full ride. The door opened on the

5th floor, Juli got off, and made her way down the corridor towards the offices of *Unterhaltung Taglich* or *Entertainment Daily*.

"Hallo Juli!" the sweet young receptionist greeted her as she glanced up from her computer.

Juliana gave her a bright smile and an amicable wave as she removed her mittens, pulled out her phone from her coat pocket and started flipping through texts and emails as she slowly made her way to her cubicle.

"Juli! Can you come into my office?" her chief editor called as she passed his corner office.

Juli doubled back and peeked inside. "Hallo Peter! You want to speak to me?"

Still at his computer typing, he nodded and gestured for her to take a seat across from his desk. She slipped her phone back into her coat pocket and looked up at him with an eager grin, giving him her full attention. Peter Muller was in his late 50s, tall and broad, a beast of a man with silver hair cut short in a trendy style and a thick well manicured beard and mustache to match. He never dressed like a business professional, tailored suits, not his style. Instead, he opted for designer jeans, converse sneakers and concert t-shirts, making him look hip and youthful.

As she waited for him to finish, she unraveled her scarf, unbuttoned her pea coat, slipped out of it, and set it on the chair next to her as she smoothed down her brown corduroy skirt and picked at a piece of lint that clung to the sleeve of her favorite fitted black H & M sweater. She looked up to see Peter watching her, an amused look on his face as he was obviously waiting for her to get comfortable before he spoke. She gave him a sheepish look, knowing he was a busy but patient man, and he flashed her a smile, his blue eyes crinkling at the corners with well-earned smile lines.

"I have an article assignment for you I think you'll find exciting." He said with a grin, as he rose from his chair and rounded his desk, a piece of paper in his hands. Leaning against the side of his desk, he crossed his long legs casually in front of him and, even though he towered in front of Juli, there was nothing intimidating about Peter. "The Rolling Stones are coming through this weekend, as you know." She nodded, the concert a highly anticipated one. "And they have this new indie rock band from Canada opening for them. They're a band that blew up online about two years ago, when some concert footage was posted on YouTube."

Juli shifted in her seat, eager excitement washing over her. "That does sound interesting. I love Canada! Did you know I did an exchange to Canada for a year when I was 16? It was this pretty little town, near the centre of the country, called Primrose, Manitoba."

"I remembered you mentioned it once, and that's why I thought you would be perfect for this story. Prairie Sound originates from the same area, and I believe a member still lives there," he said, glancing at the piece of paper in his hand with information on the band and its members. He leaned over, handing it to her as he added, "Layne Stark, the bass player, grew up in Primrose."

Juli looked up quickly, her eyes widening at the name. A name she thought she would never hear again. A name she wasn't sure she ever wanted to hear again. *Layne Stark.* She glanced down at the paper, a picture of the band at the bottom. All the boys she knew so well now grown into handsome men. Her eyes roamed over the members, all so familiar. Scanning the picture, her eyes landed on the handsome blonde next to the lead singer. *It's him, my Layne. Although he isn't my Layne, at least not anymore. He made that very clear the last time we saw each other.* Juli cleared her throat, trying to shake off the bittersweet memories that were flooding back and swallowed down, trying to temper the rush of emotion as she looked at a now curious Peter and feigned a smile.

"Layne and I went to school together." She answered simply.

"Excellent!" he exclaimed, clapping his hands together. "Then you should find the story an easy one. We want the story to focus on their quick rise to stardom via social media, and I would love a background story on each of the members. This will be a "guy next door goes famous" kind of story. It should be inspiring."

"I can do that." She replied, paper clutched in her hand as she got up from the chair and reached for her coat and scarf.

"I'll send you all the details in an email and the concert is on Friday, so you have four days to prepare. I've spoken to their agent, and he's expecting your call to make all the arrangements with the Band. I'll have a backstage pass for you and a media pass plus a ticket to the concert. Ideally, I would like you to follow them around for the day, see how they prepare, and get a good feel for who they are as a band. I want you to immerse yourself in their music so you can write your best piece." Peter outlined, making his way back around his desk and taking a seat in his chair as he looked up and met her eyes, pinning her with his steely gaze. "Depending on what you hand in, Juli, this could be a featured article in next week's publication."

Juli's pulse quickened at that. In the year that she had been at Entertainment Weekly, she had yet to land a featured article. "Thank you for this opportunity, Peter," she replied with a smile as she turned to exit his office.

Juli settled in her cubicle, her mind a mad rush of thoughts and memories. *Layne Stark. Strong boy. The boy that refused to try. The boy that said he loved you, then took it all back. The boy that took something sacred and special and then broke your heart into a million pieces.* She looked down at the paper and gripped it firmly in her hand. Layne's face, as handsome as she remembered, but now older. Not that of a boy anymore, but that of a man, with hard edges and defined angles. A man with whom she had a score to settle. She swallowed down the disappointment and frustration she felt when thinking about him as determination rose in her chest. She knew what she needed to do. *Go in there, get the interview, then get some answers. Get the closure you deserve after eight years of wondering why.*

* * *

PRAIRIE SOUND EXITED the van that was hired to transport them through the city and looked up at the large five floor brick hotel with a bright pink glass door that glowed in the dim light of the early evening. Having been in Europe for two weeks already and jet lag was no longer a concern, all of them emerged alert, eager and excited about this next adventure. They chattered as they entered the hotel to be met with a modern, almost futuristic lobby with green pods for seating and blue, white, and green swirls covering the walls toggled with pink patterned walls as contrast.

"What planet have we just landed on?" Rex asked, as he surveyed the décor. "This place is fucking crazy."

"Very spaceship chic." Steve deadpanned, making everyone laugh.

They approached the check-in desk and gave their names to the concierge. Fully checked in, with their key cards in hand, they found the elevator that took them to the 5th floor and quickly found their rooms. Rami and Layne sharing a room and Steve and Rex sharing the room across the hall. Entering Layne looked around at the simple setup, not unlike other rooms they shared in other cities, very minimalistic and modern. Quintessentially European, he decided.

Layne rolled his suitcase to one side, an artistic swirl wall splitting the two sleeping areas of the room. He was immediately grateful to not have to share a bed with his bandmate, shaking his head as yet again, the queen bed was two single beds pushed together to make one. Nothing like rolling over and falling into the dip between the mattresses. It reminded him of being a kid and going on road trips in their family's old station wagon. He would always get stuck in the middle of the backseat between his two older sisters, having to sit on the hump between the two seats. He internally laughed at the thought, the memory a truly uncomfortable one.

As the youngest of three kids and the only boy in the family, his two older sisters were more like his second and third mothers than siblings. Having been born as almost an afterthought when his mother was in her 40s, his closest sibling was already 13 when he was born and before he was 10 years old, it was just him left at home to be doted on. Having been raised on a country property a few miles from Primrose, the house he grew up in was a cute and compact, three-bedroom bungalow, but the property was expansive giving him lots of room to ride his bike, climb trees and scrape his knees.

His sisters, now in their late 30s, were both married and moved away with families of their own, so it was just him left to be close to his parents who now lived in a 55 plus development complex in St. Augustine. His parents, having moved from the homestead when he was 20, agreed to keep the property, setting up a lease to own for him so he could one day own the property outright. He loved where he lived and had dreams of building onto the home where he and his wife and kids could live happily.

Wife and kids. You need to actually date to have those. Layne self admittedly wasn't much of a dater and his entire social life revolved around Prairie Sound. If they weren't doing a show, they were rehearsing. If they weren't rehearsing, they were writing or planning out their next show. The little spare time he allowed himself, he spent alone. Hulled up in his cute little country home that was calm and eerily quiet. Over the years, he had brought in roommates periodically, but they all moved on quickly. Even his bandmate and best friend Rami had lived with him once, before he and his now fiancée,

Savanah, moved in together. Savanah was an amazing woman, and he loved seeing his best friend so happy and in love. Despite this, if he was being honest, it made him envious too. He wanted what Rami had and every time he thought about his future, his mind drifted to the one that got away, Juliana Roth.

He shook his head, dispelling the thoughts running through his mind as he set his suitcase in one corner and sat down on the bed, bouncing once to test the softness of the mattress. "Hey, what's on the agenda tomorrow?" he asked before getting up and coming around the partition where Rami was hoisting his suitcase onto the bed.

"The show is tomorrow night, so we have rehearsals late morning and apparently, we have an interview with some local entertainment reporter tomorrow morning over breakfast. She's meeting us downstairs at 9 a.m. and is going to follow us throughout the day," he said. "It's supposedly a piece on our viral success as a band."

"Cool." Layne answered with a shrug. "Could be fun."

Rami nodded and surveyed his friend, cocking his head to the side to analyze him before he asked. "Are you going to try to get in touch with her?"

Layne was surprised by his question as it had been years since he talked to Rami about Juli, as usual, keeping his thoughts and emotions to himself. He opened his mouth to respond, but Rami spoke first, halting any outgoing protests or excuses.

"I saw your face when we got the tour schedule and Hamburg was on the list. I know you thought of her immediately," he said with a wary smile.

Layne walked over to the window and looked out on

the dark street below. The glow of green and pink light from the building sconces illuminated the cobblestones in front of the hotel.

"I would be lying if I said I haven't thought about it," he replied simply. "But I'm sure she doesn't want to hear from me."

"Do you know that for sure? I know you look at her social media all the time, Layne." Rami chided, causing Layne's eyes to dart in his direction. "I lived with you for a while and have seen you do it. I also know you have pined for her for the past eight years and you've never moved on from her completely. It doesn't take a rocket scientist to see that you still live with regret about how things went down. Juli is the one that got away."

Layne turned his gaze away from his friend, feeling emotion rise as he stared back down at the darkened street below and spoke low and clear. "Juli's not the one that got away. She's the one I drove away because I was young, scared, and stupid." His mouth settled in a grim line as the familiar sting of unshed tears burned behind his eyes, his voice solemn and resolute. "In the end I treated her like she meant nothing to me and let her leave Canada, thinking I had never cared about her." Rami approached him and set a supportive hand on his friend's shoulder and Layne let out a long exhale before he turned his eyes to meet Rami's compassionate gaze. "What if she still hates me for what I did and for what I said?" he asked, feeling a combination of apprehension and emotion rise in his chest and constrict his throat painfully.

"You'll never know, unless you see her again and when else will have this opportunity?" Rami asked with a shrug.

"If anything, you can rid yourself of the guilt and offer her a much overdue apology."

Layne considered Rami's advice. *Should I reach out to her? Rami is right. When will I be in Hamburg again? Likely never. Now may be the only opportunity I have or will ever have to apologize and hopefully make things right.* Layne pulled out his phone from his back pocket and found her social media profile as Rami gave him an encouraging smile. Clicking the message icon, he typed, *Hi Juli, it's Layne* and hit send.

* * *

Hi Juli, it's Layne, Juli read the message over and over again. Four simple words running like a loop in her head. Waging an internal debate on whether to respond or simply ignore his out of the blue message. *Why, after eight years, is he reaching out now? Did he honestly expect a response?* Perhaps he is 'thinking oh, yeah, I know someone from Hamburg' and it expecting me to answer sweetly with *"Oh Layne, I'm wonderful, and you? It's so fantastic hearing from you after you broke my trust and stomped on my heart." Think again.* There was no way she was going to respond. The shock he was going to have tomorrow was going to be satisfying enough. She could already visualize it. Walking into the hotel, and she's the entertainment reporter they're expecting to follow them around all day. *Will he be sheepish? Will he be indifferent? Will he ignore the elephant in the room?* Juli wanted him to feel the animosity that she still carried. The hurt that plagued her through every relationship attempt since he broke her young and fragile heart. Juli stiffened her back and lifted her chin with determination. She was going to be professional, aloof, and not let those warm brown eyes thwart her mission. *You got this, Juli. Layne Stark won't know what hit him.*

CHAPTER 2

It was the first day of his senior year at Primrose High School and as on most first days, the school parking lot was a jumble of school buses, vehicles dropping off kids and students unsure of where to find the student parking spots along with Teachers making a desperate attempt to direct the chaos. A veteran at this already, Layne parked his car in the student parking area and got out of his vehicle, begrudgingly grabbing his backpack as he dragged his heels across the lot.

Last year of high school, he was more than ready to move on with life. Most of his friends attended St. Augustine Regional School, including his bandmates Rami, Steve, and Rex, so he wasn't excited about the upcoming year here in Primrose. Having grown up in this small community, he knew most of his class, having gone to school with many of them since kindergarten, but they were mostly acquaintances to him, so he was prepared for another year ahead as the class loner. If he was being honest, that label didn't bother him. He was a self-declared introvert and preferred the company of only a few, which pretty much just included his band. The only time he enjoyed being around others was when he could get lost in his music on a stage playing for a crowd.

Entering his English class, Layne passed his classmates, most of which were excitedly talking about their summers, a few offering him a compulsory wave or smile as he claimed a seat at a table for two near the back of the room. He hated being up front and would much rather fade into the background, acting as more of a prop than a person. Besides, Layne was a good student, got mostly A's and stayed out of trouble, so he didn't feel like he needed to be front and center in the class.

Layne dropped his backpack to the floor by the desk with a thud and started rummaging through his bag to find the notebook and pencil case he threw in there the night before. A sweet melodic voice sounded beside him, making him look up from his task in surprise.

"Hallo."

"Hello." he replied, his eyes quickly taking in the beautiful girl in front of him.

"May I sit with you?" she asked, her accent thick and familiar and her large expressive brown eyes hesitant and questioning.

His eyes meeting hers, he tried to speak, but his words scrambled in his head as he surveyed her. She was taller than average, slim but curvaceous with wispy medium length dark brown hair that framed her face and the most extraordinary doe-like brown eyes he had ever seen. She slowly blinked at him, her lashes dark, long, and lush as she waited for him to respond.

"Ah...yeah...sure." he finally managed to croak out, internally groaning at his lack of game.

She took a seat beside him and unravelled a long, thin, colorful scarf she had around her neck and stuffed it into the backpack. She pulled out a binder and a pencil, setting it neatly on the table in front of her, and let out a long exhale. He stole a glance at her, but his eyes fixated, not wanting to look away. *She's so pretty.*

She caught his glance and turned to him with a friendly smile as she put her hand out in greeting. "I am Juliana Roth. I am on an auchtauche..." she began, each word carefully said before she corrected herself. "...sorry, exchange from Germany."

Germany. She's from Germany and an exchange student. He turned to face her, offering her a kind smile. "Ich kann ein bisschen Deutsch sprechen." Layne responded, making Juliana's eyes light up.

"Sehr gut. Sorry I need to try English, very good." she nodded with approval, her eyes dancing with delight.

"My parents are German, and we speak German at home all the time. I can't speak fluently but they speak it around me enough that I understand it and can say some things," he replied in explanation.

"Good. Then can you help me? I need to speak English, but I think in German, so it is, how do you say... difficult?" she added, scrunching up her nose adorably.

He nodded, finally finding his pencil case, and setting it neatly in front of him as she had. He turned his attention back to her and put out his hand in greeting. "I'm Layne Stark."

"Stark! Stark means strong in my country. Are you strong?" she asked, as she boldly reached over and grabbed his bicep, giving it a squeeze. Then she let out the cutest giggle and took his offered hand. A zing of electricity surged through his hand, and he looked at Juliana, who seemed to notice it as well. Her eyes flashed at him through her long lashes, as a playful smile slowly curled up her lips. Her hand still holding onto his, lingered there a moment, neither noticing until Layne looked down at their hands and back up to her impossibly beautiful face, her brown eyes now twinkling with delight as she declared, "I think we will be friends, strong boy. My friends call me Juli."

CHAPTER 3

PRESENT DAY

*L*ayne followed his bandmates through the hotel lobby to the large cafeteria style breakfast area at one end of the building. The area was bustling with tourists and families as they surveyed the abundant breakfast offerings, each of them loading a plate and then finding a quiet corner to enjoy their meals. One of the great things about touring in Europe was that not everyone knew who they were, so they could enjoy a little anonymity with breakfast rather than disruptions or fanfare.

"So, who's this reporter chick that's supposed to be interviewing us?" Rex asked, shoving half a pancake in his mouth.

"I don't know exactly, but apparently, according to our agent, she knows who we are and should be meeting us here any minute now." Rami replied. "All I know is she is doing a feature article on us for a popular publication called *Entertainment Daily*."

"And she's following us around all day?" Steve asked, picking up his coffee, taking a sip and wincing at the strength of it.

"That's what I was told." Rami replied.

They all talked about the show tonight, enjoying their breakfast as Layne pulled out his phone, clicking into social media. *No message requests and no response from Juli. It's silly to think I could just show up here in her city and expect her to simply be thrilled that I'm here. It's silly to think she would even consider a reunion.* Scolding himself internally, he slipped his phone back into his pocket, feeling a wave of disappointment drowning him. Rami met his vacant gaze and offered him a half smile. Layne responded with a defeated shrug.

"You must be the Canadian band, Prairie Sound?" a sweet melodic voice asked in a thick German accent. A familiar voice. Layne's eyes darted up as his gaze met the beautiful eyes of the girl he could never forget. *Juli. She's here.* Her glance was brief, but sharp as a knife, and tinged with an aloof flash of recognition before she brought her attention over to Rami, Steve, and Rex.

"I am not sure if you all remember me, but I remember you." She said confidently, offering the three men her sweet smile. "I did a student exchange to Primrose many years ago, and we had a chance to meet."

Rex, recognizing her, piped in, pointing to her and then to Layne, "Hey, I remember you. You and Layne were hot and heavy back then!" Rex, not always good at social cues, let out a gruff chuckle at the irony.

Rami groaned and shook his head as heat rose up

Layne's neck and settled in his cheeks. Juli glanced back to Layne again, narrowing her eyes and giving him a look of pure distaste. "Layne." she said coldly, chin high as she clasped her hands in front of her. She turned her gaze back to Rex and replied, "Yes, that was me. Juliana Roth, but please call me Juli." she said, shaking each of their hands in turn but stopping at Layne with hesitation, obviously at war with herself to stay professional. Layne tried to will himself to speak, but he was so mesmerized by seeing her again that no words could come out. Although eight years had passed, she was as beautiful as he remembered. Her face, having lost the softness of teenager hood, was more defined and mature, making her look impossibly gorgeous and womanly. With a dry mouth, he swallowed down hard, knowing he needed to say something, anything, but all he could muster was a quick nod and a choked, "Hello, Juli."

Ever the professional, she put out her hand, and he met her icy gaze as he reached out, accepting her greeting. As his hand slipped into hers the familiar zing of electricity sparked between them, just as it had the first time they had met. His eyes flitted up to her expressive eyes, a combination of surprise and something he wished he would never see again flashing in their depths. *Hurt. She's still hurt.* At that realization, he wanted to wrap her up in his arms and tell her he was sorry for every lie he told, but he kept his eyes locked on hers, refusing to leave her gaze. A few awkward seconds passed between them until she released his hand, looked away nervously, and cleared her throat as she gestured to an empty seat at their table. Enraptured by their exchange, Rami, Steve and Rex collectively nodded for her to join them as she took a seat and offered a smile to the rest of the band, her smile never reaching Layne. Settling her rucksack on her lap, she untied it carefully and pulled out a notebook and pen, setting them neatly on the table in front of her. Something about this little gesture felt like déjà vu and made Layne think of the first day of school. *She's the same girl, My girl.* That seemingly possessive thought made the voice of reason inside his head internally chide him. *She's no longer your girl, Layne. You made sure of that the last time you saw her.*

SETTLING her hands on her notebook, Juli glanced between each member, her eyes quickly drifting over Layne as she started, "I am from a popular entertainment publication called *Entertainment Daily*. We are not a gossip magazine, but a magazine that publishes quality articles about pop culture. I solely write about music, what is hot, what is trending, things like that. We are interested in your story and in knowing how social media played a part in your success," she explained. "Tonight is the concert and I am going to follow you throughout the day. Ask questions, see what your process is to prepare and speak to you after the concert too. I plan to write the article over the next few days, and will you be available for any fact checking over the weekend?" she asked as she opened her notebook and glanced at some notes on the page before looking up to meet their gazes. "I understand you are to take a train to Munich on Monday morning?"

Rami, as the lead singer, usually took the lead with the media, offered her a nod and a smile. "Yes, that's right. We have a few days to explore the city and then we're on to Munich."

Juli mirrored his smile. "Now I have some basic questions to get started before we all go to the venue." She informed, readying her pen. "I understand two years ago a video went viral on YouTube and to date has been viewed more than 10 million times." She said, checking the facts in her notebook. "What was that like to suddenly be seen by so many people worldwide?"

"Surreal. I think the guys would agree it was overwhelming at first. We went from being a popular local band, still playing bars and local festivals, to suddenly national, then international." Rami answered.

"And did you have a social media following before the video that started this?" she asked, taking notes in her notebook.

"Very little." Steve answered. "We were more focused on the music and although we had social media, we weren't using it to our advantage."

Rami nodded in agreement as he explained. "A friend took some concert footage from a local concert and she, along with Layne, uploaded it to YouTube. The videos went viral so quickly, I don't think any of us were fully prepared for it. Layne is now in charge of our social media content for the band," he replied, giving Layne a nudge in the arm.

Juli looked at Layne, her eyes narrowing incredulously, and he flashed her a modest smile. Her gaze darting away, she looked down at her notebook as she asked, "And do you have any social media training or experience? Are you an influencer?"

Rex let out a rough laugh. "Layne is far too quiet to be an influencer. He prefers to be in the background."

"It wasn't hard to figure out once we started." Layne replied simply.

"Layne is probably the smartest guy I know. He had the algorithms and trends figured out in a flash. I think he took a social media marketing course as well." Rami added, looking to Layne for confirmation. He nodded, his gaze drifting over to Juli. She seemed to be avoiding eye contact with him, but he couldn't look away. *I can't believe she's here.*

"I understand the first video was of you, Rami, singing to…" she looked at her notes and continued, "…a girl with pink hair?"

Rami laughed, and the other guys joined in. Layne stayed quiet, his eyes locked on Juli.

"Yes, that's my fiancé, Savanah. We just got engaged and are planning to get married next summer."

"That is so nice. Congratulations." Juli replied sweetly and cleared her throat again, Layne literally seeing her mind working overtime on how to phrase her next question. Looking up from her notebook and glancing at Rex and Steve. "Married? Girlfriends? Partners?"

Rex and Steve both shook their heads. Her eyes slowly moved to Layne, full of curiosity but attempting aloofness. "And you?" she asked him.

"I'm not seeing anyone," he replied, not faltering her gaze.

Juli let out a quick breath, then looked down at her

notebook, taking a few quick notes as his bandmates' mirthful eyes caught his. A smile tugged at Layne's lips. *Was she trying to find out my status? Perhaps she's not as closed off as she appears.*

JULI SELF admittedly was being bold, asking that last question. Her blatant attempt at fishing for information not lost on the men around the table. Selfishly and curiously, she wanted to know, even if she was angry and still felt the pain of Layne's rejection all those years ago. Seeing him here today, his melting chocolate eyes locked on her, brought back feelings she wasn't expecting. Raw emotions she had pushed down for years, telling herself that what they experienced together was just two dumb kids getting their first taste of adulthood and none of those seemingly big feelings at the time were real. Juli got the reaction she was hoping for upon their reunion. A satisfying little shock and awe when he first saw her. However, what she wasn't expecting to see was the sadness in his eyes. A deep-down remorsefulness that didn't match the words he said to her the last time they spoke. Like if given the opportunity, he would take back everything that he said.

She straightened her spine and raised her chin, determined to not let his soft gaze derail her. *Layne will not get off that easy.* She had been waiting eight years to give him a piece of her mind. To have the guts to confront him the way she should have all those years ago, and she wasn't going to waste this opportunity. Tonight, after the concert, after she got her story and before she walked away and out of his life forever, they were going to talk. Really talk, and she was going to make sure he knew how deeply he wounded her.

She glanced over at Layne, his eyes darting to meet hers. He was still handsome, his face the same, but now mature with sharper angles and a sexy facial scruff that she thought added to his handsomeness. His brown eyes were still the same too, so soft and warm. A cozy blanket wrapped around her broken heart. A glimmer of pain in his gaze unsettled her, so much so that she needed to look away. *I am not going to feel sorry for him as there was no reason for what he did.* Taking a quick breath, she wrote their statuses in her notebook and proceeded with her questions, getting all that she needed to build the foundation for her article.

"I think it's time for us to go," Rami said, glancing at his phone. "Our driver should be here soon to pick us up for sound check. I know I need to go back to the room to get a few things."

As they all rose from the table, Juli grabbed her notebook, stuffed it back into her rucksack and replied, "I will wait in the lobby. Is there room for me to travel with you?"

Rami nodded his head, and the entire band made their way to the elevators. Juli claimed a pod in the front entrance and turned to watch them go. Layne glanced her way, giving her a wary look, like if he let her out of his sight, she may disappear again. In a way, she wished she could disappear. Just forget she even came here and go home and curl up in bed and cry. If their first encounter was any indication, she had a feeling deep down in the pit of her stomach that today was going to challenge her resolve. *Can I handle spending the day with the boy, now a man that I still consider the love of my life?* Juli wasn't sure, and she had no choice but to find out.

CHAPTER 4

EIGHT YEARS AGO

*L*ayne couldn't get the beautiful exchange student out of his mind. She was everywhere. In the halls, in the gym, everywhere he turned, she seemed to be there. Even with her in a grade below him and only sharing one English class with each other, he would find her stealing glances and exchanging coy smiles from across the room. *She's just so pretty*, he'd think as he watched her from the back of the classroom, animatedly chatting with classmates. She had said hello to him many times over the past month, but they had yet to have a full-fledged conversation. He wanted to, and several times he tried, but she was always whisked away by her exchange partner and the other girls in her grade, leaving her to simply give him a quick smile or quiet 'hallo' in passing.

Today, he sat on the bleachers at the intramural basketball game happening in the gym. Several other students dispersed amongst the rows, cheered for their friends and classmates. Layne wasn't interested in the game, but it was better than finding a classroom or corner to wait out his lunch hour. *Who needed an hour break, anyway?* As a student who pulled out good grades and generally remained at the top of his classes, he would fill the pause in his day by quietly completing his homework wherever he could find some quiet. However, with it being the beginning of the school year, there wasn't much homework to be had, so he conceded to watching fellow students toss around an orange ball. A mind-numbing sport, in his opinion.

"Hallo, strong boy." Juli's melodic voice sounded as she slid in next to him, bumping her hip to his as she did. She was dressed in a pair of boyfriend jeans, rolled up at the ankles, a baggy brown sweater, her signature colorful long skinny scarf wrapped around her neck and black combat books on her feet. Her style retro grunge. Not like the other girls her age, who were all glossed and primped, looking like they just walked out of Sephora.

He straightened his posture at the sight of her, his pulse thrumming at her proximity to him. She had a distinctive spicy vanilla scent that swirled in the air around her, making his senses tingle with the awareness that she was next to him. "Hello." he answered, liking the way her leg so casually brushed against his.

Juli turned to face him, her big brown eyes twinkling with mirth as she jutted her plush lips out in a pout and stated. "You never sit with me in class. I want to talk with you."

Layne looked down at his hands. Juli was bold, bolder than most girls he knew. He glanced up at her, his eyes roaming over her beautiful makeup free face and realizing she was sitting so close he could make out the light freckles that dappled the bridge of her perfect nose. "I want to talk with you too," he admitted. Layne generally wasn't a flirt or used to girls pursuing him. Most of the girls at school he had known since kindergarten and were more like sisters or cousins than love interests. With Juli it was different though. "What do you want to talk about?"

"I want to know about you," she said, curling her fingers around his bicep and giving it a squeeze. "Do you play sports?" she asked, looking towards the basketball players running up and down the court.

He let out a big guffaw and adamantly shook his head, making her giggle. "No, I never really cared for sports, but I do like music, though."

"Music!" she exclaimed excitedly. "What kind of music?"

"Rock mostly, but I like almost anything. I play bass guitar in a rock band, so mostly the music we play," he answered, offering her a wistful smile.

"Oh, you are a musician! Do I know the songs you play?" she asked, leaning in closer to him and making his head swirl with her intoxicating scent.

"Probably. We play Bon Jovi, Coldplay, Arcade Fire, U2, music like that."

"My Chemical Romance?" she asked, curiously. "That is my favorite!"

"Welcome to the Black Parade. Great tune," he replied, impressed, and a little surprised by her taste in music. "Do you listen to Rage Against the Machine too?"

"Yes!" she exclaimed excitedly, pulling out her IPod from her pocket and a long string of earphones. "Do you want to listen to my music?"

He smiled, as she handed him one side of the earphones and she took the other side, slipping it into her ear. He leaned his head closer, feeling her warm breath brushing over the side of his face as Nirvana came through and Layne gave her a sideways glance and an approving grin. She mirrored his smile, and his heart jumped in response as they filled the empty hour with conversation and music.

CHAPTER 5

PRESENT DAY

*J*uli waited patiently in one of the lime green pod chairs that graced the front entrance of the Prizeotel Hamburg-City. She glanced towards the elevator, no sign of the band yet, so she pulled out her phone, opening her social media and clicking on Layne's message to her again. He really did look so incredibly surprised when he saw her. She wanted that element of surprise. Maybe knock him off his game a bit and fluster him. He deserved it. He deserved what he was going to get from her today.

"The other guys will be down shortly." A familiar voice said, startling her and making her scramble to close her social media messages.

She looked up into Layne's warm brown eyes, and he gave her a sweet smile. A smile that used to make her melt. *Had he seen me looking at his message?* Juli cleared her throat nervously, the thought bothering her more than it should as she stood up from where she was seated and adjusted the rucksack on her shoulder. An awkward silence fell on the pair as an unmistakable heat radiated across the few feet between them. She hated that he looked so good. His blonde hair was longer than she remembered, sexily mussed and long enough to tug. He still dressed all casual rocker grunge, which she still found incredibly attractive. Layne hadn't changed much. Still the same boy with quiet confidence, who was now a man with an edge she instantly found sexy. *Get it together, Juli. You shouldn't be thinking about him that way. Not after how he treated you. Not after all the things he said.*

Nervously, he rocked on his heels, his shoulders high and tense as his hands sat in his pockets and he stared down at the ground. The silence was deafening and the air thick with unanswered questions and unresolved feelings. It was too quiet, and Juli's outgoing personality simply had to step in. It had no choice.

"How are you? How is your family?" she asked. *Small talk, yes, small talk is safe.*

"I'm good, it's been a crazy year as you probably know, but good," he answered carefully. "I still live outside of Primrose, on the same property and in the same house. My parents live in St. Augustine, now."

"Are they in good health?" she asked, leaning ever so slightly towards him. She always loved his parents. Both from Germany, they loved it when she came over and they could converse in their native language. They were always so kind and sweet to her and treated her like one of the family.

"Yes, they are, for the most part. I check in on them a lot and now, while away, I have a friend checking on them for me. They aren't young anymore and need my help more and more."

"And your sisters?" she inquired, still feeling in a safe zone with this catch up.

"Both married with kids. If you can believe it, I have five nieces and nephews now," he said with a smile.

Juli smiled back, thinking of Layne surrounded by little kids all wanting attention from their one and only uncle.

"And you?" Layne asked, reversing the questioning.

"Oh, my brother lives in New Zealand and my dad got remarried and lives in The Netherlands." she answered, knowing he knew her history with her parents' divorce. "My mom passed away from breast cancer three years ago. So, I am the only one in Hamburg now."

Layne's brows knit together, and his brown eyes turned to melting pools of compassion as he said, "I'm so sorry, Juli. I know you and your mother were very close."

"Till the end, yes," she replied, feeling a painful lump rise in her throat as it did every time she talked about her late mother.

A silence descended on the pair again until Layne spoke, "I just wanted to say..." he began, the elevator bell disrupting his thoughts. Rami, Steve, and Rex stepped out of the elevator and strode over to join them, just as their driver entered the building with a sign saying Prairie Sound.

"I guess that's us," Layne said, glancing over to Juli.

She caught his deflection with them no longer alone and cleared her throat with nervous frustration as she followed them out of the hotel with the driver. The vehicle waiting for them was a van and Rami, Steve and Rex all slipped into the back seat, leaving the seat for two in the middle. Juli slid in and Layne got in next to her, his leg brushing hers and making a heat instantly rise in her traitorous body. He reached for his seat belt and their eyes met as he rummaged for the buckle between them.

"Sorry, this is a tight squeeze here," he apologized, his warm breath on her face. "Let me help you."

He looked between them and continued to dig, his hand brushing over her hip. Such a small thing, but making her completely aware of him and their proximity.

"Here." he said, holding the buckle awkwardly while she stretched to connect it. Snapping it into place, they looked up, their eyes locking on each other, and something happened that she wasn't expecting. Layne's soft brown eyes looked anguished, imploring, as if tears could spring up at any moment and he whispered so faintly. She was sure only she could hear him. "I'm sorry."

Her heart twisted with those two small words and the swell of sadness and sincerity in his eyes. Those two words she craved to hear uttered from his lips said to her here in this cramped van with his bandmates watching. Words she thought may heal her heart now, making her frustrated. So incredibly frustrated. She swallowed her emotion and turned away quickly, feeling heat flush her cheeks as she leaned back in her seat facing forward, willing herself not to look his way. *I am not going to let him get to me. I am not going to let him get to me.* She chanted to herself like a mantra. *He is not going to break my resolve.*

CHAPTER 6

It had been a long school day; Layne dodged traffic exiting the school parking lot and unlocked the driver's side of his little Honda Civic. It wasn't a cool car like some of the wealthier kids in town, but it was a dependable one and he owned it outright from money he and his band had made performing over the summer. He was about to get into his vehicle when he saw Juli, walking down the sidewalk towards the East side of town, her backpack looking heavy and slung awkwardly over her shoulder. The late October weather was bitter and biting to the skin, with winter threatening its appearance any day now. He watched her pull the collar of her coat up and even from a distance, he could see she wasn't prepared for the cold.

Quickly, he got in his vehicle, immediately feeling the need to rescue her from the cruelty of her first Canadian winter. Exiting the parking lot and pulling onto Main Street, he caught up to her as she passed the Credit Union and pulled off to the side, honking his horn. Startled, she turned around, her hand on her heart, but as glimmers of recognition appeared, a grateful smile enveloped her face. He waved her over and rolled down his window.

"Do you want a ride? I can take you wherever you need to go," he offered.

She surveyed his car and met his expectant gaze through the open window; the wind picking up and making her noticeably shiver.

"Please." she said with chattering teeth as she scurried towards the passenger side and climbed in. He rolled up his window, reached for his backpack at her legs, and brushed them inadvertently when he reached for it. She gave him a coy smile, and he could feel the heat bloom on his face. Juli's eyes twinkled with mirth as she graced him with her melodic laugh.

"You are so cute," she said, noticing his embarrassment. Her comment making his face burn even hotter. "Do I make you, em, how do you say, aufgeregt?"

"Nervous? Honesty, you do a little," he answered truthfully, tossing his backpack into the backseat and meeting her gaze.

She scrunched up her nose. *She's so adorable.* "A little? I do not understand."

"It means you do make me nervous but not in a bad way," he replied, waiting for her reaction.

"You like it?" she asked, her smile growing with the question.

"I do," he replied, meeting her big bright eyes that he just realized were the color of rich dark hot chocolate. This made her eyes dance with delight as she rested her back against the seat, biting her bottom lip to keep from grinning.

Pulling back onto Main Street, she directed him to her destination, a blue bungalow on the corner. He pulled into the driveway, pulling right up to the garage door. She unbuckled her seatbelt and turned to face him, her eyes twinkling as she said, "I like you, strong boy." Then unexpectedly she leaned in and gave him a quick kiss on the cheek, surprising him and making the heat return where her lips had touched. Before his thoughts could process, Juli let out her sweet giggle, grabbed her backpack, and exited his vehicle, giving him a final wave along with a flash of her beautiful smile as she disappeared into the house.

Layne sat there a moment, unsure of what had just happened, but instantly wanting it to happen again.

CHAPTER 7

EIGHT YEARS AGO

*J*ust one ride, rescuing Juli from a cold walk home was all it took for Juli to find her way to his car every day after school. They had been doing this ritual for weeks and Layne wanted to ask her out so badly, but everyday he internally kicked himself for chickening out. *Today is going to be the day.* His inner voice coached him as he leaned against his car, trying to look cool and nonchalant as he waited for her. *You're just going to casually see if she has plans this weekend and suggest maybe you hang out. Maybe listen to music.* An idea popped into his head, and he brightened as he saw her walk out the front of the school towards him as he admired her. A colorful knit toque slouched on her head and made her wispy dark hair curl out around the edges and frame her pretty face. She bounced cheerfully when she walked as her black combat boots made deep marks in the freshly fallen snow.

"Hallo, my strong boy." She said, reaching out, squeezing his bicep and coming into his space. *It would be so easy to just lean in and kiss her. Perhaps take her off guard the way she surprised me a few weeks ago with that kiss on the cheek.* His eyes darted to her pillowy pink lips, wanting so badly to taste them. She must have noticed his lingering look as she stepped back and offered him a sweet smile.

"Your chariot awaits," he said, feeling high on her presence as he came around the vehicle and opened the passenger door for her.

"You are my knight in shiny armor." She replied with a playful giggle and brushed her hand over his arm as she got in. She had this way of always touching him when they were around each other. Light touches he was sure were innocent in intent, but from her made him very aware of his body's reactions to them. He would never consider himself a touchy-feely kind of person, but when she did it to him, all he wanted to do was reciprocate. *But would she like it if I did?* Her affectionate touches were an extension of her. A part of her friendly personality he was sure she didn't even think about. *If I were to reach out for her, touch her hand, her arm, her leg, her face, would she see it as unwanted?* He was determined to find out.

He climbed into his car and turned to smile at her. A damp strand of hair clung to her rosy cold cheek from the winter wind. Reaching over, he tucked it to the side, his fingertips softly brushing the hollow of her cheek. Their eyes met, and hers twinkled with approval. *Those eyes. I could get lost in those eyes.* He swallowed, his mouth dry as he glanced down at her lips, so full and welcoming. *I want to kiss her right now.* As if sensing what he was thinking, she turned to face the front and let out a long, nervous exhale. *A deflection, but not a rejection.* The realization of that emboldening him more. He started his car and glanced back at Juli, who was looking out the window, a smile tugging at her lips. *She is enjoying this.* This slow burn of attraction between them.

He pulled out of the parking lot and turned onto the main street. *Go for it, just go for it* his inner voice chanted. *Ask her out!* "Juli, do you have any plans this weekend? I was wondering if you wanted to come to my house on Saturday. I have band practice and thought you might like to hear us play."

Juli turned her head, her face instantly brightening, and a huge smiled blossomed on her beautiful face. "Yes, I would like that," she said excitedly, leaning into him.

Feeling reassured by her reaction, he boldly put out his hand, palm up and open to her. He glanced briefly to see her reaction as she brought her bottom lip between her teeth and slid her fingers between his, their hands lacing together. The feel of her hand in his made sparks fly inside his head and butterflies take flight in his belly. In that moment, simply holding her hand made it feel like they were dating. Like they were a thing. This moment feeling like the beginning of something special.

PRESENT DAY

"There it is, Elbphilharmonie Hamburg." Juli said, gesturing over to the venue, appearing a few blocks away. The building stood out like a beacon with the bottom of an old brick warehouse and the top a modern glass structure resembling waves on the water. It was a masterpiece of architecture situated on the peninsula of the Elbe River. "We in Hamburg call it Elphi."

The entire band leaned in, marveling at the structure before them. "It's beautiful." Layne said, taking in the interesting building they were approaching.

"Indeed. A little old with the new." Juli replied, pulling her press pass out and slipping the lanyard around her neck. "Some of us like it, some don't. It has been a bit controversial."

Layne wanted to know more about it but put a pin in his questions as something he would research later. Glancing over to Juli, who was looking at her notebook, he wondered what she was doing over the next few days and how he was going to get her to spend those days with him. As much fun as it would be to explore the city with his bandmates, he would so much rather spend those few days with her. *Would she even want to?* Her entire reaction to him today told him it was just a pipe dream, or perhaps it was just his self-deprecating attitude rearing its ugly head again. When he whispered, he was sorry. It was a knee jerk reaction. Not exactly the way he imagined saying it. He just felt an overwhelming need to just get it out before they interacted any further. *I just need a chance to explain why I did what I did. We need a chance to talk alone so I can get everything off my chest and tell her how I feel. At least if I can get her to sit down with me and give me an opportunity to explain, she can decide for herself if she wants to spend time with me.*

Pulling into a private entrance at the back of the building, a couple dozen fans stood by the entrance guarded by huge security guards.

"Check it out!" Rex rasped, pointing towards a girl screaming and holding a sign that said "Ich liebe Prairie Sound."

"Nice." Steve replied, bumping Rex's fist.

"Your videos are very popular in Germany." Juli shared, turning to face the guys in the back. "They like your sound, the indie rock vibe, your handsome faces. There will be lots of excited fans just here to see you. To them, you are the main act." She added, as she caught Layne's gaze and looked away quickly, clutching her knapsack.

They pulled into the private parking lot at the back of the building; the driver bringing them straight to the door. As they exited the vehicle, a man stepped forward with a clipboard and was flagged by two hulking security guards.

"Hallo Prairie Sound. I am Dierk and I will guide you through to the dressing room." He glanced over at Juli, a look of confusion on his face. "Is this a girlfriend or family?"

Juli held up her media pass, and he looked it over, frowning and shaking his head. "I do not have you on my list, Ms. Roth."

"She is with us," Layne spoke up. "She's writing an article on us for *Entertainment Daily.*"

Dierk looked at her pass again, pulled out his cell phone, dialing quickly and gestured one of the security guards over as he explained to Juli, "I will take the band to their dressing room, and we will find out if you are permitted to be here Ms. Roth." Dierk informed as he took the call and handed the cell phone over to the security guard.

Layne turned to his bandmates before they followed Dierk. "You guys go ahead, and I'll stay with Juli. I'll make sure she can get in, okay?" They nodded, and he turned to Juli, a confused look on her face.

JULI STARED AT LAYNE, a confusing mix of frustration at the situation and appreciation at his thoughtfulness at staying by her side. Watching the band disappear through the doors of the building, leaving her and Layne alone with the two rather large and intimidating security guards, one of which appeared to be arguing with someone on the phone. She glanced at Layne and said, "You did not have to do that. I am fine waiting here."

"I have no doubt you'd be fine, Juli, but I didn't want you to be alone," he answered, glancing at the large men and then meeting her gaze. "Besides, we don't have to be on stage for at least an hour for sound check."

Why does he have to be so nice? She questioned, slightly unnerved, as she pulled out her phone and started texting. Firing off a text to Peter, she stared at her phone for a minute, willing him to answer, and let out a deep, exasperated sigh. Knowing Layne was watching her, she glanced up at him and explained. "Usually, these things are figured out before I get here."

"Do you do a lot of these types of interviews?" he asked curiously.

"No, this is my first expose on a band. I mostly attend concerts and do reviews, but this is my first feature piece." She shared. "Or at least I hope it will be. I have only been in journalism for a year now."

He nodded as her phone dinged with an incoming text. She read it, smiled, and strode over to the security guards, showing them. A security guard pulled out his phone and within a few minutes, Dierk returned with an apologetic look on his face.

"I am so sorry," he said. "Ms. Roth, you have full access, but you must stay with the band, otherwise I or one of my colleagues will usher you to and from your seats. We do not allow the media to roam free backstage in any restricted areas."

She nodded, knowing the drill and so happy this was figured out. Juli flashed Dierk her sweetest smile as she touched his arm in thanks. Juli was very aware that she had always been defined as friendly, but not until she was an adult did she realize that her natural outgoing nature wielded her some power over the opposite sex. She had the power to soften a situation with a little harmless touch and some flirting, and wasn't above using that power to get what she wanted. Dierk's face immediately softened, and he brazenly looked Juli up and down, as if truly seeing her for the first time. He flashed her an approving smile, obviously liking what he saw. Letting go of Dierk's arm, she turned to see Layne, his face flushed, and his eyes dark with envy. *He is jealous.* And with that realization, a small, maniacal part of her smiled wickedly. *Good. Serves him right.*

"Will you take us to the back now?" Juli asked, sweetly batting her eyelashes almost comically to play up the flirtation for her audience. She was laying it on thick, but the reaction Layne was giving off was far too self satisfying.

"Come with me," Dierk said, putting his arm out to Juli. She looped her arm into his and he led them through a long, brightly lit corridor that brought them to private dressing rooms. "This is you," he said, gesturing towards the door that was labeled Prairie Sound. "I will come in..." he quickly glanced at his watch. "...45 minutes to bring you to the stage for your sound check. All your equipment is set up for you on stage already."

Layne nodded his thanks as Juli disengaged her arm from Dierk, and he gave her one more long, unapologetic look up and down before Layne stepped between them, breaking his unabashed perusal. Surprised at Layne's reaction, Juli stepped back but couldn't see the look Layne gave Dierk. She could, however, see Dierk's reaction, a white-faced acknowledgement he better back off as he turned quickly on his heel and hurried down the corridor.

Layne slowly turned around, his eyes blazing with fire, and her heart jolted as their gazes locked. Instantly heat rose on her cheeks, not from embarrassment but from her body's reaction to his primal show of dominance and possession over her. Her belly coiled and core clenched, making her pulse quicken at the intensity. The Layne she had known was laid back and calm, so this alpha show was beyond unexpected. Layne stepped forward, crowding her against the wall beside the dressing room door, the heat of his body so close making her breath hitch as he opened his mouth to speak. She brought her hand up, covering his lips with two fingers and pleading with her eyes for him to stop. The last thing she needed was for him to say something, anything that might make her lose her resolve and disintegrate her self-control. Layne closed his mouth and backed away. No words shared between them as he got himself together. Juli tried to catch her breath, shaken, like she had been tossed in a whirlwind, needing a moment to control the incessant thrumming of her heart. They stood there a moment, eyes locked on each other as the tension between them waned. Layne reached for the door, the intensity in his eyes having softened and the expression on his face sheepish. He flashed her an apologetic look, quickly breaking their eye contact as he opened it, gesturing for her to enter. Swallowing down the lingering tension of the moment she entered the room, Rami, Rex, and Steve all lounging on a large plush sectional in the middle of the room, sipping from glass bottles of Coca Cola. Layne passed her approaching a beverage and food table and picked up two bottles, uncapping them both and handing one to Juli. She accepted his offering, neither daring to make eye contact as she claimed a seat in a sleek leather chair across from the couch.

Layne took a seat next to the guys on the couch and Juli smiled, taking in the scene, a perfect picture for her article. "Do you mind if I take a few photos today?" she asked, opening her phone. The guys all nodded, and she lifted her phone to snap a candid photo of them lounging on the couch. "That is a nice one." She said, admiring her photo and putting her phone down on the coffee table. "I have some more questions before you go on stage." She pulled out her notebook and pen, flipping it open.

"I am curious how it has been, being a part of a large tour? I read you have been on tour with Aerosmith now, The Rolling Stones."

"Yes, with Aerosmith we opened for them on their North American tour this past winter and spring." Rami answered for the band.

"Was that your first experience touring?" she asked curiously.

"It was," Rami answered. "One of the nice things about being part of a large tour is there are roadies that do the grunt work for you. No need to lug around equipment or instruments. You just show up and be ready to entertain."

"And you spent many years taking equipment with you?"

"We would have to haul drums, keyboards, guitars and

often, depending on the venue, have to haul amps around with us as well." Steve added.

"And where do you practice and prepare for your shows?" she asked.

"Layne's garage right now, but my fiancée and I are looking for a property where we can build a new studio for practicing and perhaps even recording."

The garage. A flood of memories of that garage instantly came back to Juli. The first time he brought her to his house. That feeling of awe as she watched them play, completely enamored with Layne. The very garage where they first kissed, where they spent hours making out and where she... Juli shook her head at the thought. If those walls could talk. Her face flushed at the memory and her eyes darted to Layne. His gaze met hers, knowing exactly what she was thinking of.

CHAPTER 9

EIGHT YEARS AGO

*P*ulling up to the blue bungalow on the corner, Layne recognized this home as the residence of the Parkers, Mr. Parker, one partner from Estes & Parker Law Firm whose office was on main street Primrose. They had a daughter, Lisa, in 11th grade, Juli's exchange partner, that Layne knew well, despite not hanging out in the same social circles. That was the thing about being a part of a small town. Everyone knew everyone.

Knocking once, the door flew open, Juli's twinkling eyes and impossibly beautiful smile greeting him. "Come in." She said, gesturing to enter the front entrance. He stomped his feet at the door, knocking off any snow that accumulated on his boots, and entered the home. Mr. and Mrs. Parker stood there, their smiles wide and friendly.

"Hello Layne." Mr. Parker said, putting his hand out to shake.

Layne mirrored their smiles, took his offered hand and Mr. Parker squeezed it hard, making Layne's eyes dart up in surprise to meet his gaze. With one stern look, a mutual understanding passed between them, the look of a father telling him to handle Juli carefully.

"I'll bring Juli back safely, Sir." he said, swallowing down hard, his message to him loud and clear.

Mr. Parker let go and his wife slapped him on the shoulder playfully, letting out a laugh. "We know you will be Layne. Please say hello to your parents for us."

He nodded and glanced at Juli, who had already gotten her coat and boots on, her eyes dancing with amusement at this parent vs. suitor power exchange.

They exited the house and Juli immediately reached for Layne's hand, lacing her fingers with his. A smile tugged at his lips, liking this newfound affection between them. She swung their arms, her body buzzing as she exclaimed, "I am so excited to hear you play!"

He glanced at her, feeling excited too. Juli radiated so much warmth and joy, he was sure it might melt the snow around them. When he was with her, he couldn't help but be consumed by it. She was like a light in an otherwise dim room. Opening her door, she gave him a dreamy look through her long lashes and with a sweet smile; she went on her tiptoes to kiss him on the cheek. She beamed at him and slid into the car. Closing her door, he touched his cheek, feeling the heat rise under his fingertips as he grinned from ear to ear.

PULLING into a driveway on a large country property, Juli looked around, seeing a cute, pretty, little white house surrounded by trees. The house looked like a storybook cottage, warm and inviting, and instantly she felt at home. She glanced at another structure that was detached from the house with a single overhead door. *That must be the garage.* Several cars were parked in the driveway, two of which were in front of the building.

He pulled right up to the side of the detached building and put his car in park. "This is where we practice. My parents have allowed us to turn it into a bit of a studio." She nodded, eagerly unfastening her seatbelt. "Some of the guys are here already."

Juli got out of the vehicle and Layne met her halfway, taking her hand in his as he led her to the side door, opened it and gestured for her to enter. Juli's eyes widened as she took in their practice space. It was larger than she expected. The walls were painted army green with band posters hung up haphazardly. On the floor was a patchwork of makeshift flooring made from a spongy material that connected like puzzle pieces and covered the cold concrete of the garage floor. Along one wall was an old couch that looked very well loved, a couple of bar style stools and in one corner was a drum set, keyboard, and a bunch of guitars, both acoustic and electric. Amps flagged the instruments in the corners.

Two boys looked up from their instruments and smiled at her as they came over to greet them.

"Layne, I wondered why you weren't around when I got here," a boy with shoulder length curly dark brown hair said as his eyes settled on Juli. "I now know why."

The other boy was very tall with a deeper complexion and long black straight hair. He quietly smiled at them both, waiting for introductions. Both boys had kind, curious eyes and Juli instantly felt comfortable around them, despite being outnumbered by the opposite sex.

"I am Juliana Roth." she said, putting her hand out to them in greeting, shaking both of their hands and offering them her sweet smile. "But call me Juli, please."

"This is Rami Perez, our lead singer." Layne said about the boy with the curly hair. "And this is Steve Furgallo. He is our keyboardist," he said, gesturing to the boy with the long straight hair.

"Where are you from?" Rami asked, curiously. "You have a strong accent."

"Hamburg, Germany. I am here for a year on a student exchange."

They both nodded and turned their gaze to Layne, Rami giving him a sly wink as the side door flew open and another guy walked in, followed by a petite blonde girl, hot on his heels.

"I know, I know, I'm late!" the boy, dressed in a leather rocker jacket, ripped jeans, and black The Clash T-shirt. His hair was shaved on the sides with the top long and styled in a mohawk. Juli had seen her share of mohawks before, but what stood out was the color. Dyed a brilliant bright blue, it made his indigo eyes pop out. He glanced at the blonde that was with him and she cocked an eyebrow his way, her blue eyes dancing mischievously. She was pretty, petite, and slight, dressed in a red puffy jacket, and tight black skinny jeans, her blonde hair pulled up in a messy ponytail.

"We know exactly why you were late, Rex," Steve said with a shake of his head and a laugh.

The boy with the blue hair pulled the blonde girl towards him and planted an unapologetic kiss on her lips, then let her go with a waggle of his eyebrows as she stumbled back, looking wobbly on her legs.

Layne rolled his eyes and turned to Juli. "This is Rex Johnson, our drummer and his girlfriend, Harlow Ford. Rex and Harlow, this is Juli Roth."

"Ah, okay, so this is the girl you can't stop talking about Layne. I can see why," he said, giving Juli a once over and putting his hand out to bump Layne's. Before turning back to Juli and giving her a playful wink.

Juli turned to Layne, her eyes sparkling with amusement, and she noticed the heat of embarrassment bloom in his cheeks as she asked, "You talk about me?"

Layne's eyes darted to Rex, and he glared at him, giving him a look to say, "shut up" and turned his gaze slowly to Juli, admitting, "I have mentioned you to them."

Rex let out a gruff laugh as he taunted, "Juli is so pretty, Juli is so smart, Juli, Juli, Juli."

Harlow smacked Rex on the chest and furrowed her brows at him. "Leave him alone, Rex. It's nice to see Layne liking someone, and it's nice to have another girl to talk to. Too much testosterone in this garage."

Juli smiled at Harlow instantly, liking the little blonde firecracker of a girl. Harlow looped her arm in Juli's and led her over to the couch to take a seat. As the guys organized themselves for practice, Harlow chatted with her effortlessly, asking her questions about Germany and her exchange, but Juli's eyes kept drifting over to Layne. He kept stealing glances at her, his brown eyes sparkling and a constant smile tugging at his lips. *He is so cute.* A quiet confidence and endearing boyish charm that appealed to her.

"Let's start with "Smells Like Teen Spirit." Rami finally said, his bandmates nodding as they played. Rami stepping to the microphone as he sang out the first line. Juli wasn't sure what she was expecting, but it wasn't this. *They are so good.* Something telling her she was witnessing the beginnings of greatness. Completely transfixed, she glanced towards Layne, bass guitar slung around him, looking effortlessly cool and the corner of his mouth twitched up into a lopsided smile as her teenage heart swooned.

CHAPTER 10

PRESENT DAY

The band was directed to the stage and Dierk guided Juli to the seats in the front, where she could get a good view of their sound check. Flashbacks of the first time she saw them play in Layne's musty, cold garage studio came back to her, and she smiled nostalgically. Even then, she could see they were on the cusp of something incredible. Prairie Sound had come so far and seeing them on this huge stage, the guys were pretty much the same as she remembered, and knowing where they came from made her chest fill with pride. These humble Canadian boys were living their dream. Feeling inspired, she pulled out her notebook and started writing. The words poured out on the page, knowing the exact angle she was going to take with this story.

Looking up, she glanced over to Layne and couldn't help but feel a wistfulness while she watched him. He carried himself with the same quiet confidence that she fell in love with when she was just a teenage girl with stars in her eyes. Confusion clouded her thoughts. Part of her wanted to hate him, considering what he had done to her and leave him at the end of the day, hanging with unanswered questions the way he had left her. But after his show of dominance outside the dressing room and watching him now, she couldn't help but be intrigued by the man he had become. Still coming across as the sweet guy she remembered, only now there was a protectiveness towards her she found both surprising and wildly attractive. As if he had staked his claim, and she still belonged to him. *So, if he cared for her, why did he break things off with me the way he did and completely shatter my heart?* The Layne she thought she knew didn't have it in his nature to hurt someone; she could see that clear as day. *So why me, then? Why did he break things off so unceremoniously, leaving me confused and heartbroken?* She glanced his way again, Layne's eyes darting over to meet hers, a slow smile tugging at his lips. As much as she didn't want to, she couldn't deny she had missed that smile.

THERE WAS something so satisfying about looking out into the empty concert hall to see Juli watching him. Over the years Layne had thought about this so many times he had lost count. A long-standing fantasy of performing and one day looking out at the crowd to see her big brown eyes staring back up at him. Juli starred in all his fantasies, though. Every time seeing her and reliving all the amazing moments they spent together. Her year in Primrose ungrained in his consciousness as the best year of his life.

His eyes darted to her, and she met his gaze, a feeling

of hopefulness blooming in his chest. There was still something there. He felt it today with each tiny interaction and he could see by her reactions that she felt it too. The brush of his leg against hers in the van. Their encounter in the hallway. The way her breath hitched at his closeness. Those walls were up high though, and to bring them down, he had his work cut out for him. He just needed a chance to explain, tell her what he was thinking and why he said what he said to her. He just needed a moment alone with her to make things right. *But will she let me explain? Will she give me a chance?* She had her heart under lock and key, and he had to figure out how to pick the lock.

CHAPTER 11

EIGHT YEARS AGO

ayne followed Juli as she walked around the garage, touching the instruments, perusing the band posters thoughtfully and taking in everything around her. She picked up his guitar pick he had set down on a music stand and was flipping it between her fingers nimbly. The little movement, mesmerizing.

"I like your space," she said, her lips curling into a smile as she took in the AC/DC poster on the wall and walked over to the drum set, hitting the cymbals lightly. Striding over to his bass guitar, she crouched down, ran her fingertips over the strings and glanced up at Layne. "Can you teach me?"

"Sure." he said, reaching for the guitar and handing it to her, gesturing for her to lift the strap over her head. She settled the guitar in position and looked over to him, a huge smile on her face as she asked, "Now what?"

"May I show you?" he asked, his eyes questioning. She nodded eagerly. He positioned himself behind her, his face at her ear and he took a quick self-indulgent inhale, letting her spicy vanilla scent fuel him. Noticing goose-bumps rise on her skin, he swallowed, their proximity making him so aware of her body and his own. "Put your fingers here," he rasped out, setting her left hand on the body of the guitar, positioning her fingers on the strings. "And then you take your right hand and position your hand like this," he said, bringing her hand under the neck of the bass and positioning her fingers on the strings. He guided her fingers with his own to press down on the different strings, creating different pitches.

"This is difficult." She said with her melodic giggle.

"It takes some practice." He replied, stepping back, and helping her lift the guitar over her head, setting it gently on its stand.

Juli strode over and sank onto the couch with a long sigh, and he followed, taking a seat at the opposite end. Noticing how far away he sat, she frowned and shimmied herself next to him, bridging the gap between them. She turned to face him, her hand settling on his knee. His body was buzzing, never having had a girl be so forward, but not wanting to overstep her boundaries. He turned his body to face her and reached up, tucking a tendril of her soft dark brown hair over her ear, letting his fingertips run down the soft length of the strands and down the side of her face. Her breath hitched, and she swallowed as their eyes locked on each other, her looking at him like he hung the moon. *Kiss her, kiss her.* His internal voice was chanting as he glanced at her lips. He swallowed too, feeling a nervousness settle in his belly, his heart pounding like a beating drum.

"Can I kiss you, Juli?" he asked quietly as his eyes darting up to meet hers.

"Yes." she whispered, her voice coming out breathy.

Layne reached up and slid his hand around the back of her neck, running his fingers into her hair, and tentatively came closer. She closed her eyes, her long lashes fanning out as he took one last look at the beautiful girl in front of him and brushed his lips to hers, soft and saccharine. She let out a sigh into his mouth as he savored the softness of her lips on his. A feeling he had never experienced before, yet instantly knew he wanted to feel again, surged through his body as he pulled her closer. Their lips moved timidly, each exploring this connection with caution, yet not wanting to step too far. They kissed like this for a while, not keeping track of time or place until a knock sounded at the side door that startled them both. They sprang apart, Juli on one side, and Layne on the other, both of their faces flushed red.

"Layne." A sing song voice called and an older woman, in her 60s stepped inside. She was short, stout, had red ruddy cheeks, warm brown eyes just like Layne's, and a bright smile. Her hair was short and wispy, a beautiful silvery grey. She held her hand to her heart and looked from Layne to Juli on the couch as she said, "Layne, I saw your friends left but I didn't realize you still had someone here." She said, offering Juli a kind smile. "I was just calling you in for dinner."

Layne stood up from the couch. "Danke, Mama." he said, going over to her, as she pulled him in for a side hug. "Mom, this is Juliana Roth or Juli. She's an exchange student from Hamburg, Germany, and she's living with the Parkers."

"Oh, my goodness!" Mrs. Stark exclaimed as she approached Juli, who had risen from the couch to greet her. "You are so pretty, sehr hubsch!" Mrs. Stark exclaimed, taking her hands in hers. Juli beamed at his mother as she pulled her in for a hug and chided Layne. "You didn't tell me you have a girlfriend."

With his mother's words, Layne's eyes darted to Juli, and she responded with a look of delight as she addressed his mother. "I am his girlfriend, yes, and it is nice to meet you, Mrs. Stark."

Warmth washed over him at her words. *Juli wants to be your girlfriend.* He looked at Juli, her eyes meeting his, a look of knowing passing between them. A silent agreement that this is what they both wanted. "Yes, Mama, Juli is my girlfriend."

His mother looked at him, her face painted with pure happiness as she turned to Juli again. "Then you must stay for dinner. I'm making Layne's favorite, schnitzel and spaetzle."

"It is my favorite too!" Juli said, moving over to Layne and reaching for his hand, threading her fingers with his.

His mother looked at them both again, a look of approval on her face as she gushed, "Such a beautiful couple." She strode to the door, gesturing for them to follow her. "I hope you two are hungry."

CHAPTER 12

PRESENT DAY

With the sound check over, the band made their way backstage and back to the dressing room. Dierk guided Juli to the room after them, his demeanour no longer flirtatious and more professional. She walked inside and thanked him, touching his arm again, and Dierk's eyes flitted to Layne, who instantly narrowed his gaze as he watched their exchange carefully. *Why was Layne being jealous so incredibly satisfying and why did she like it so much?* Paying him no mind, she strode towards the couch where the band was lounging again.

"That was wonderful!" she exclaimed, sinking into the same chair she claimed before. "I love your original music! I know some of our readers will be curious about your writing process, so I have some more questions for you."

They all nodded as she flipped open her notebook and clicked her pen as she glanced at the page; a heart drawn in the corner. Little subconscious doodles, something she had always done when processing her thoughts. Her eyes drifted to Layne and quickly back to her notebook and questions. "Tell me your process of writing your original songs. Is it collaborative, or do you each have parts that are yours?"

"Mostly collaborative. We all come up with lyric ideas." Rami answered. "Mostly, Layne and I write the lyrics, though."

Her eyes drifted back to Layne, his mesmerizing gaze meeting hers as he answered, "Our last single, "Love Lost" was written by me." She had heard the song before, but never made the association, but now, the lyrics coasting through her mind, she knew who that song was about. Her eyes met his intense stare confirming her suspicions, and her heart inadvertently did a flip flop.

"That was our first ballad to climb the charts." Steve added. "Layne is good at bringing a strong depth of emotion to songs. He may be quiet, but there is a lot floating around in his head over there."

Juli knew this to be true and hearing this from his bandmate made her think about all the times she wished he would be more forthcoming with his thoughts. So many times, when they were together, she could literally see his mind going a million miles a minute. A chronic overthinker. *Was that what he was doing when their relationship ended? Overthinking how they could keep it going?* This realization never entered her mind until now. She glanced at Layne, his eyes seeking hers, their gazes meeting, and a profound knowing passing between them. This whole time, she played the scorned victim in their tale, but something in his eyes was telling her that there was more than what was on the surface. More behind the scenes.

The overwhelming need to talk to him and hear him out now overtaking her.

Dierk peeked into the dressing room, breaking her from her whirling thoughts. "Your driver is here to take you back to the hotel. We will see you back here at 6 p.m., okay?"

They all rose from their seats and reached for their jackets, quickly dressing and following Dierk down the corridor from which they entered the building. The band climbed into the van, Layne and Juli sitting together again. This time, as they sat next to each other, it felt different, like some cloud was starting to lift, and a better understanding was forming. Juli's mind was going around in loops, trying to figure out how she was going to get time alone with Layne to talk. She needed to process this realization and get him to speak candidly. She needed to make sense of it all.

THEY PULLED up to their hotel, Juli exiting the van, followed by Layne and the rest of the band. They made their way towards the entrance and Layne felt a warm hand curl around his arm, halting him in his tracks. He looked down to see Juli clasping his bicep, her brown eyes wide and imploring. The other guys stopped too, watching them with curiosity.

"Can we go somewhere and talk?" she asked softly, a deep well of emotion behind her tone.

Layne nodded and gestured for his bandmates to go ahead without him. Rami clapped him on the back, giving him an encouraging look as he followed Steve and Rex. Layne turned to Juli, her expressive eyes reflecting a multitude of emotions as he asked softly, "Where did you want to go?"

Her eyes darted around, seeing a café down the street, and she gestured over to it. He nodded in acknowledgement as he followed her, no words passing between them as they walked, the anticipation of this conversation making the air thick and heavy. Ducking into the little café, a mixture of baked goods, coffee and French fries swirled in the air, making Layne instantly hungry. Spotting an empty table in the corner by the window, Juli strode over and took a seat to claim it. Layne sat down across from her, a waiter rushing over to greet them and hand them each a menu.

"Are you hungry?" he asked, unsure of what to say, his mind still trying to catch up with this turn of events.

"I am," she replied, putting down her menu and offering him a sweet smile. He felt like a balloon being let go, her smile instantly making the pent-up tension whoosh out of his body. Giving him hope.

The waiter returned, and they placed their orders, two orders of French fries and Cokes, and as the waiter scurried off, Juli leaned back in her chair, glancing out the window at the people walking by. Layne watched carefully as he waited patiently for her to speak first. He didn't have to wait long.

"I wanted to speak to you privately," she started, turning her gaze to him, her brows drawn together and a mix of sadness and determination in her eyes. "I need you to listen and let me get out everything I have to say and what I have felt for a long time." Her lashes fluttered, unshed tears glistening in her baby browns.

He nodded, swallowing down hard, a painful tightness settling in his chest and constricting his throat as he listened, hoping for the best but expecting the worst.

"You hurt me, Layne." she began simply, her words like daggers to his heart, as she leaned forward, ensnared him with anguished eyes and pointed to her chest. "You broke my heart. I was hopelessly in love with you, and we had experienced so much together. So many firsts. It was a special time for me, our year together. A time I have never forgotten, even after all these years. A time I sometimes wish I could forget because it ended so painfully."

The deep piercing pain in Layne's chest rose into his throat, forming a lump he couldn't swallow away. Her words and the excruciating pain in her voice was too much. The tightening made him want to bury his head in his hands and sob, but he didn't deserve the relief of a cathartic cry. He deserved to look into her pain-stricken eyes and hear each heart wrenching word she had to say.

She looked towards the window again, blinked rapidly, a tear escaping the corner of her eye and rolling down her cheek.

Without a moment's hesitation, he stretched over the table, his thumb wiping the tear away and his palm lingering gently on her cheek. She turned, her eyes meeting his, pure agony in their depths as she asked. "Was our time together not special for you?"

He retracted his touch, her question twisting the dagger deeper. *How could she think that? How could he even describe to her how much their time together meant to him?* It was hard to put into words, but he needed to try. This was his one chance to tell Juli how he felt, to perhaps erase what he said the last time they saw each other. "It meant everything to me Juli." he said in a ragged voice. "It was the best time of my life."

"Then why would you say, "It was fun, but I don't feel the same way?" she asked, fingers up air quoting him verbatim. "You said you didn't think we should try as it didn't mean as much to you as it did to me." she threw back, fire in her eyes, burning him down to the ground.

His harsh words that day were so ingrained in his brain and hearing her quote them reminded him how incredibly cold and aloof he had come across. How in protecting himself and in an attempt to protect them both, he, through his actions, made her feel like she had been discarded. There was only one way to answer her question, though. Pure honestly the only answer. "I was scared, Juli."

"I was scared too, Layne." she shot back a look of frustration on her face. "I was so scared of going home, back to Hamburg, and never seeing you again. But I knew I needed to try, as it is not everyday you fall in love. When you said those things to me, I felt like you had lied to me. Like you had taken advantage of me and my naïve heart. I gave everything to you. Everything." she repeated, enunciating the word as her voice cracked under the emotion. "The way you treated our time together and the things that you said to me that day, has plagued every attempt I've made at finding someone since. I always question myself and what they say to me. I can't allow myself to trust anyone."

He put his elbows on the table, running his hands through his hair as he hung his head, not able to look into her anguished eyes anymore. As painful as their breakup was for him, the realization that he had permanently scarred her and made her question her judgement was way worse a penance than the self-loathing and loneliness he inflicted on himself. "I am so sorry," he whispered. "I was selfish. I tried to protect my heart but hurt you instead," he confessed as his eyes, shiny with tears, rose to meet hers. "I couldn't imagine life without you, Juli. You consumed me. I was so in love with you that the thought of not being able to see you every day was unfathomable to me. It was a pain my inexperienced heart wasn't ready for and at the time, I felt like I was protecting myself and you by pushing you away. I am so incredibly sorry, Juli." Her eyes softened with his admission, but wariness still remained in their depths. "I was an immature, inexperienced idiot and if I could take back those words I would, in a heartbeat."

"You were an idiot." She agreed, an unexpected smile tugging at her lips.

"A huge one," he emphasized, putting his hands out wide, his face getting serious again and his brows drawing together as he pinned her with his remorseful stare. "I have thought about you every day for eight years. Not a single day has gone by where I don't wonder what you are doing and where you are. Not a day has gone by where I don't wish I could take all those terrible words back."

Juli stared back, searching his gaze for truth. Finding what she was looking for, her big, beautiful eyes grew wide as saucers, tears hovered over the brim as she admitted in a whisper. "I have thought of you, too."

They sat there in contemplative silence, their words lingering between them, both staring into each other's eyes until Layne broke the silence with a question. "Can I spend the next two days with you? I want to get to know you again, Juli. Even if it is just as friends."

His question seemed to wash over Juli, and he could see her mind warring with her heart. She let out a long exhale as she steadied her words, answering. "Yes."

CHAPTER 13

EIGHT YEARS AGO

Word got out quickly around Primrose High that Layne and Juli were dating. Layne, usually the unassuming guy at the back of the classroom, was now the focus of attention by boys and girls alike. The girls seemed to be noticing him for the first time and the guys, giving him nods of approval as he passed them in the hallway. Although he found the attention a little unnerving, he didn't care, as he had Juli on his arm. When she smiled at him, touched his arm, kissed him, he felt like he was the luckiest guy in the world. She had a way of always making him feel like he hung the moon, giving him dreamy looks of pure adoration that he didn't know if he deserved, but he couldn't help but enjoy.

Layne rummaged through his locker, looking for his ever-missing pencil case, when a pair of arms wrapped around his waist and Juli's spicy vanilla scent captured his senses. She hugged him from behind, her cheek on his back, making him smile. He reached for her hands, unraveling them from his body, and turned to face her. Her eyes danced playfully as he leaned down and kissed her chastely before he asked, "Do you want to go to the movies on Saturday?"

"Yes." she replied excitedly with a little clap of her hands. "I have not been to the movies in Canada."

"Well, then I'll take you," he said, wrapping his arms around her. "Will it be okay with the Parkers?"

She nodded, "I think so." Very quickly he had to make his intentions with Juli known to the Parker family, who had taken on the responsibility of her care while here in Canada. Mr. Parker, ever the interrogator, needed to know where they were going and who they would be with and had even talked to Layne's parents to ensure he was respectful with Juli. Of course, only the two of them knew how much time they spent making out on the garage couch. In his opinion, what they didn't know wouldn't hurt them.

Layne picked up Juli, and after giving Mr. and Mrs. Parker the required rundown, they drove to St. Augustine. Pulling into the parking lot of the theatre, he opened her door, playing the doting boyfriend. He figured out quickly that Juli liked it, so if she liked it, he was going to do it. Taking her hand, they walked into the theatre, the line up already dwindled. He let her pick the movie, and after a quick stop at the snack counter for popcorn and candy, they made their way into the theatre. The theatre was already half full and Layne spotted two seats in the upper corner that were more secluded from the rest. They settled into their seats, Juli resting her head on his shoulder and looking up at him sweetly with her doe eyes and long lashes.

"The way you look at me makes me crazy," he confessed with a smile tugging his lips.

"Crazy?" she asked, sitting up to turn towards him. "How do you mean?"

He laughed, as she was so impossibly cute, with her thick accent and the way she scrunched up her button nose when she didn't understand something.

"I mean, you make me... well...you...I'm not sure how to describe it." he said with a shrug.

"Do you mean I turn you on?" she asked. "I think that's how you say it."

He nearly choked when she asked, reaching for his cola to take a sip. She kept looking at him, still bewildered and looking for clarification. He swallowed down, unsure if he should just come out and say it, boldness not in his nature. "Yes, like that."

"Oh!" she said, looking lower, her eyes quickly darting up. "Do I make you unbequem?"

"No, you don't make me uncomfortable. You make me very comfortable," he replied. "I like it when you are...friendly with me."

"Like a girlfriend?" she clarified. "Affectionate?"

"Yes, that's the right word," he replied.

She smiled and leaned in, stealing a kiss. Pulling away, she held his gaze. "I like being your girlfriend, and I like you, my strong boy."

"I like being your boyfriend," he replied, sliding his hand behind her head as he did when he wanted to kiss her. That move was her kryptonite, and she would melt every time. Bringing his lips to hers, he kissed her softly and tenderly and she kissed him back, moving her lips with his. Kissing Juli was quickly becoming one of his favorite things to do, and he never wanted to stop.

CHAPTER 14

PRESENT DAY

*J*uli unlocked the door to her apartment and stepped inside, putting her keys in a bowl on her dinette table. She had three hours until she had to meet Prairie Sound at the hotel, opting to drive again with them to the venue. Resting her back against the door a moment, she closed her eyes, her mind racing from her long overdue conversation with Layne. Layne, owning up to what he said to her, how he broke her heart and apologizing. She had wanted to hear this from him for years, their relationship never getting the necessary closure for her to move on. Even though the conversation did have a sense of finality to it, she still didn't feel settled with what happened between them today and agreed to spend the next two days with him. What happened between them during their year together was so much more than two inexperienced teenagers falling in love. They had experienced something deeply profound that some people never get to experience in a lifetime. True love.

Her mind drifted to a conversation she had with her mother before she passed away. She and her mother were best friends, two peas in a pod and closer than most with their mothers. She shared everything with her, and she was there when she returned from Canada, helping to pick up the pieces of her shattered heart. Closing her eyes now, she could see her mother's face so pale and frail as she gripped her hand and whispered through shaky breaths, "Juli, my dear daughter. If you are lucky enough to find your way back to the man you love, don't let him go. Take it from me when I tell you this: live your life to fullest, sacrifice for what you want and who you want. And when you have them, love them with all you have, hold tight and never let go. I did not do that with your father, and it is my deepest regret."

She had never known exactly why her parents had split up, but she did know her mother never stopped loving her father. In many ways, she could tell her father never stopped loving her mother too. Both had such strong personalities, they could never compromise, neither willing to sacrifice for the other. Even with Juli and her brother Lukas involved, they were never able to make it work. Then, when her mother got sick, she finally saw the love they once shared manifest again. Her father made special trips to help with her care, and when she passed, he was inconsolable. She didn't want to live her life with that type of regret. The type of regret that plagues you for the rest of your life.

She had so many regrets already, far too many for someone only 24 years old. She would not let Layne be one of them. Not anymore. She was going to give him a chance. Even with her apprehension, her heart still guarded, she was going to try to open up to him again and see what happens. The decision made she walked straight to her bedroom. She had a concert to get ready for.

* * *

Prairie Sound waited in the lobby, their ride coming soon to pick them up for tonight's concert. Layne rocked on the heels of his combat boots, glancing at his phone. He and Juli had exchanged numbers, and she had texted to let him know she was on the way.

"Are things good between you and Juli?" Rami asked curiously, the rest of the band leaning in to hear his answer.

"As good as we can be for now. There's still a lot to talk about, but she has agreed to spend the day with me tomorrow, at the very least."

"Ditching us for a chick. Good on you man," Rex said, nodding his head, his eyes darting to the front entrance and widening almost comically as he said with a low growl. "Speak of the devil."

Layne's eyes followed his sightline, and his jaw dropped. Juli stood just inside the pink glass door of the building dressed in a black leather jacket, Rolling Stones classic T-shirt, and tight leather pants that hugged every glorious curve. His eyes trailed down her impossibly long legs to see a familiar pair of worn and scuffed black combat boots, and instantly a smile tugged at his lips. *There's my girl.* Her hair was pulled up at the sides, in some gravity defying masterclass in braiding, to look like a faux hawk, and her makeup was dark and sultry, bringing out the expresso color of her eyes. Layne's mouth went dry, and all he could do was gawk opened mouthed at the smoke show in front of him.

Steve leaned in with a little chuckle. "Pick your jaw up off the floor, man."

Layne shut his mouth as she sashayed over to them, confident sway in her step and a playful twinkle in her eye. *Juli knows she looks good.* She shot him a glance, and surveyed the others quickly, then brought her eyes back to Layne, locking him with a sultry stare.

"You look amazing." Layne said, not knowing if words could adequately describe how incredibly hot she looked.

"Danke. Do I look like I should be hanging out with a bunch of rockstars?" she asked, holding out her arms and doing a slow turn.

The entire band nodded, and Rami nudged Layne, giving him a sly thumbs up. With that, their driver entered the hotel lobby, and they followed him to the van. The same seating arrangement applied the band in the back and Layne and Juli sliding in next to each other in the middle.

Juli reached to connect her seatbelt and met Layne's eyes. This time, instead of giving him a look of anger and animosity, she gave him a look of reassurance that they were okay. She reached for his hand, and he could feel the tension in his shoulders ease as a wave of relief washed over him and she laced her fingers with his. Staring down at their hands, fitting so perfectly together, he glanced her way, her lips parted ever so slightly, letting out a quiet exhale. His eyes flitted to her lips, so inviting, wanting nothing more than to kiss her again. *Not here, not in front of the guys. I need to have her alone.*

* * *

JULI COULD NOT DENY the heat between her and Layne, the spark sufficiently back and burning bright. The look he gave her when he saw her, dressed all hot and sexy, like a badass vixen, was exactly what she was hoping for. She knew she had gone a little over the top, making herself look a little extra for tonight, but the satisfaction of seeing his face was all she needed to fuel her. After an afternoon of deep thought and decision making, she had decided she was going to give Layne a chance to redeem himself in her eyes and that she was going to do her best to open her heart to him again. What that looked like now, she was unsure, but she was ready to find out.

Arriving at the venue, a large crowd of fans screaming by the parkade entrance greeted them as they entered. They all got out of the vehicle and Dierk met them, his eyes immediately zoning in on Juli and flashing with pure appreciation. Layne possessively reached for her hand and Dierk noticed his eyes going from Juli to Layne and to their connected hands. Nodding resolutely, he led them to the back, the sound of music and the audience forming in the auditorium, humming through the backstage. Something about that sound felt like the definition of anticipation and excitement, and it made her pulse quicken.

Dierk led them into the dressing room, telling them it

was 45 minutes till show time and telling Juli he would be back in 15 to bring her to her seat in the front row.

"May I ask you a few more questions?" she asked, knowing despite the mounting excitement of showtime, she still had an article to write. They nodded as she pulled out her phone and clicked on a recording app. "May I record you? No notebook tonight."

"Of course." Rami answered, getting comfortable on the couch.

"I want to know how you feel just before a show starts and what it feels like to get on that stage."

"It is exhilarating." Rami replied.

"Fucking awesome." Rex added.

"Literally there is no feeling like it," Steve mused.

Juli brought her gaze to Layne, his mind obviously formulating his answer to her question. "It feels like falling in love." he replied simply.

Juli was taken aback by his answer, but pressed further. "Falling in love, how so?"

"When you fall in love, you feel your heartbeat wildly in your chest, you feel so acutely aware of your surroundings and the person you are with, and you feel like you can conquer the world." He replied, looking down at his hands, a smile tugging at his lips as his eyes slowly drifted back to her, meeting her raptured gaze. "That's what performing feels like. Like you are in the perfect place, at the perfect time with the people you want to be with," he said, looking towards his bandmates, their smiles wide. "It's falling in love with your music every single night and feels like nothing is more amazing than that moment together on stage."

A quell of emotion rose in Juli's chest and tears pricked her eyes. His words were like poetry to her heart.

"Now do you see what we mean when we say Layne has a way with words?" Rex exclaimed. "Fuck, Layne, you brought a tear to my eye," he sniffed, feigning wiping tears from her face.

Everyone laughed, Juli included as she turned off her recorder and leaned back, relaxing in the chair. The perfect ending to her story. Her eyes floated dreamily over to Layne as their gazes met, both knowing at that moment they had turned the page, and she was ready to write their next chapter.

CHAPTER 15

Five months. They had been dating five months and although to most couples five months would seem insignificant, to Layne, it felt momentous. For five months, he lived in a world where Juli consumed his every thought. With this being his senior year, he was grateful he was a good student and completing his work in class, because when he wasn't in class, he was either with Juli or talking to her. They were inseparable. As per her exchange family's request, they only spent Friday night and Saturday together. Leaving weeknights and Sundays for time with the Parkers. He had no problem following the rules, but what they didn't know is that they would text each other for hours every night, and on their lunch hour they would sneak behind the school, ducking away into the thick tree line to make out where they couldn't be seen. They could so easily get caught, but so far no one was the wiser and he made the most out of every second with her.

After every weekend practice, they would find themselves on the couch, exploring each other and pushing their boundaries. Although they had not been intimate, the way she kissed and touched him, and encouraged him to touch her, the possibility of them taking their relationship to a sexual level seemed inevitable.

He slid his hand under her sweater, his hand grazing the underside of her bra and savoring the feel of her soft, supple skin under his fingertips. She straddled his hips, her skirt riding up to her upper thighs. His other hand in her hair as he kissed her deeply, and she rocked her core against him. Their tongues tangled deliciously as his hand slipped from her hair and settled on her behind, pressing her centre against his throbbing groin. She pulled her lips away breathlessly, her face flushed, her eyes hazy.

"You are so beautiful, Juli." he said with his other hand resting on the other side of her hips as she continued to grind her core against his growing hardness, creating a friction that fueled them both. She bit her bottom lip and closed her eyes as she unabashedly rocked over him, and he planted kisses along the column of her neck. He had never done this before, but he didn't want it to stop. His girlfriend was so perfect, moving above him. Lost in the moment, she was chasing something, and he could feel a slow burn start in his spine. Suddenly her beautiful eyes flew open, meeting him as her mouth parted, her breath catching, as she vibrated in his arms. Dropping her head to his neck, she let out a quiet moan and shuddered, her hot breath coasting over his neck. *Holy hell.* Her chest heaving against his, he ran his hand over her back, realization of what just happened, registering as they tried both tried to steady their breaths. Juli lifted her head, his eyes questioning as they met hers, hazy with lust, both satiated and flustered.

"I just..." she started as her cheeks turned red hot and she lifted her hands to cover her face.

"You did," he confirmed, peeling her hands away and cupping her heated face, forcing her to look at him as he searched her embarrassed gaze. "It's okay, Juli. It was beautiful."

"Did you?" she asked, glancing down at his lap.

"No." he replied with a low chuckle, his eyes meeting her with sincerity. "I'm not in a rush, Juli. I want to be with you like that, but not until you're ready."

"Have you before?" she asked, searching his eyes.

"No." he answered. "You would be my first."

Taking his face in her hands, she kissed him deeply, then pulled away but rested her forehead against his as she stared deep into his eyes and said, "I want my first time to be with you."

CHAPTER 16

PRESENT DAY

The concert was everything Juli expected and more and her body buzzed with that satisfying high you feel after a truly incredible concert experience. Watching Prairie for the first time LIVE on such a big stage was surreal and exhilarating, knowing she was one of the few that truly understood their transition from their humble beginnings to the rockstars they were today. The entire time they performed, her eyes were on Layne. He wasn't the front man, but you could see how much he loved to perform. He exuded an air of quiet confidence on stage that she found incredibly attractive and even though she knew he preferred to be in the background; he had a presence that stood out amongst the group. Perhaps she was a bit biased, but watching them perform he was all she could see.

After the concert, she was guided backstage down a different corridor than the dressing rooms to a larger area that was set up for a meet and greet. About three dozen fans were there already, chattering with excitement, and

Juli figured they were contest winners, likely from local radio stations. She watched as Prairie Sound posed, took pictures, and talked with their eager fans. She watched with admiration as they took the time with each concert goer, showing gratitude to them and making the experience a special one. Juli pulled out her phone, opening her notes app as she jotted down her observations along with other thoughts she wanted to capture from the experience.

"Hey." a familiar voice sounded, and she looked up to be met with Layne's gorgeous brown eyes and handsome smile. "Did you enjoy the show?"

"I loved it!" she exclaimed, looking around to see most of the fans were now gone, only a few staff lingering in the space. "Sorry, I was taking notes for the article and seemed to have been deep in thought. Is the meet and greet over?"

Nodding, Layne put out his hand to her, which she took lacing her fingers with his, as she asked, "Are you going back to the hotel, or would you all like to go out for a drink?"

"I know the guys were thinking about going out, something about the Reeperbahn and a club where the Beatles played some of their first gigs."

"Yes, the Indra Club!" she replied, having spent many a night there with friends, taking in the live music and atmosphere. "It is an old place but interesting, lots of music history there."

"Do you want to join us? I mean, I want you to join us," Layne corrected, squeezing her hand as they made their way down the corridor back to the dressing room. "I want to spend every moment I can with you, if that's okay."

Hearing him say that made nervous butterflies take flight in her belly. Such a different feeling than earlier today. "Yes, I want that too," she replied.

Layne stopped, looked around, the other band members turning the corner and disappearing down a connecting corridor. They were alone, his eyes surveying the area, and she had a feeling she knew what he wanted to do and her pulse quickened at the thought.

"Over there." She managed, pointing to a spot against the wall, hidden by miscellaneous equipment and out of the bright corridor's fluorescent lights. Dragging her eagerly along with him, until they were out of view and tucked into the shadows, he pulled her into his body. Layne was lean and strong against her, more filled out than when he was 17. Sliding his hand up to the nape of her neck, she met his gaze, dark with lust.

"I couldn't wait another second to kiss you again," he breathed out huskily, the heat of his mouth hovering over hers making her entire body sizzle and burn.

"Then kiss me," she whispered, her voice coming out strangled and needy.

Bridging the gap, he captured her lips, the intensity of his pent-up desire taking her off guard, as her body responded, melting against his. Hooking her arms around his neck, he lifted her, her legs wrapping around his body as he backed her into the corner. The hard surface anchoring her body, she pressed her core against the growing ridge pressing against his jeans. She could hardly breathe; as they passionately kissed and ground into each other, a coil in her lower belly winding tightly and about to spring back. She could feel how hard and ridiculously aroused he was as they rocked against each other, making her heartbeat pulse between her legs. Their kissing became frantic, needy, and she gasped as they found an angle, giving her the friction she needed to come undone. His mouth left her lips, finding the tender skin on her neck as he bit lightly, making a whimper escape from her throat. He brought his mouth to her ear, "Shh, I want to feel you come in my arms. The way I know you can," he whispered as he brought her earlobe into his mouth and sucked. That was all it took. Heat surging through her body, she buried her face in his shoulder and shuddered, giving into pleasure as he held her tightly and branded hot kisses and bites on her neck. Feeling a burning heat rise in her neck to settle in her cheeks, she raised her head to meet his darkened eyes, which flashed with an almost cocky approval.

"That felt very déjà vu." Juli rasped, breaths heavy and laboured.

"Are you okay?" he asked, setting her on her feet, his smile turning to concern as he touched her burning cheeks and searched her face. "I'm sorry if I surprised you or was too rough. All I wanted to do was kiss you and got a little carried away."

"I'm okay and you kissed me alright, and..." she replied, letting out a little giggle. "No one has been able to make me do that but you."

He reached out and touched her cheek tenderly as their eyes locked on each other. "It's beautiful." He said, leaning down to brush his lips softly to hers.

Voices echoed down the hall, and she pulled her lips away, burying her head in his chest. The voices trailed off. They both shook with laughter as he wrapped her up in his arms and kissed her head. "Let's go find the guys and go get that drink."

* * *

THEIR DRIVER PULLED up to the front of the famous Indra Club, the red painted facade standing out against the brick building. A part of the wall was notched out like an arched window, lined with steel bars, and flagged by posters announcing upcoming performers. Wood cutouts of an electric guitar, a man playing a saxophone, and a drum set were fastened to the bars, with the original Indra Club sign above it. The building was old and iconic, like it had many stories to tell.

There was a lineup and Juli, still wearing her media pass, approached the bouncer at the door and showed it to him. The band hung back as they watched her talk to him for a moment, her German too quick for Layne to pick up everything. She touched the man's arm, using her usual charm, and walked back over to the guys.

"We are in, come with me," she said, flashing the bouncer her sweetest smile and guiding the band into the building.

"This place is fucking amazing." Rex shouted above the live music and chatter. The club was narrow and long, with a platform stage at the far end. The gold coffered ceilings gave the room a bit more height and visual inter-est. Booths lined one wall with tables and wooden chairs and on the lower level closest to the stage, small round tables stood surrounded by the same wooden chairs. The entire room was lit dimly with red candle holders and votives, giving it a hazy red glow. Juli spotted a booth and table on the one side and gestured for them to go claim it. Taking a seat, they managed to fit around the space and had a good view of the band playing on stage.

"So, this is where The Beatles played back in the 60s." Rami said, with wonder in his eyes as he looked around and scanned over the framed pictures of the band behind them.

"Yes, they say this is the place that launched them. Apparently, they lived backstage in an old storeroom with concrete walls, bunk beds and no heat. Right next to the toilets, no less." Juli shared, curling up her nose. "The conditions were terrible, but every night they would play for seven hours straight. This was where they met Ringo Starr and brought him over to the Beatles. Lots of stories about them and this place." The guys seemed impressed by her knowledge. "I think we need to go to the bar to get our drinks. Do you all drink beer or something else?"

"Beer is good for me," Steve said and the rest of the guys nodded.

"Okay, then I will get you all the most popular beer in Germany. It is my favorite." She said, getting up and sauntering over to the bar. Layne's eyes followed the sway of her hips in those hot as hell leather pants, his eyes not leaving her behind, until he got a jab in the ribs from Rex.

"I like your girl," he said gruffly. "I remember her as a very nice girl, but now she's a total badass!"

Layne laughed, knowing that was high praise from

Rex. He smiled and glanced at Juli who was talking animatedly to the bartender. "I'm going to help her."

He strode towards the bar, hearing Juli shouting over the music, her thanks to the bartender as he set down five beer bottles. Layne took out his wallet and handed the bartender money, then grabbed three of the bottles. Juli gave him a look of gratitude as she grabbed the last two.

At the table, Rex held up the beer bottle and squinted his eyes. "What are we drinking here? Wei...hen..step...geez, I have no clue how to fucking say it."

"Weihnestephaner Hefe Weissbier" she spewed off with ease.

"Yeah, that!" Rex answered by taking a long swig, then holding the bottle out and nodding his head with approval. "Pretty good." Everyone laughed.

They hung out together at the Indra Club, till the wee hours of the morning, one drink turning to two, two turning to three. Finally, they called it a night, and they all climbed back into the van and headed for the hotel. Juli looked at her watch, 4 a.m. and groaned, her head feeling fuzzy and light from alcohol. The U-Bahn was closed, and she would have to find a cab to take her home. Layne, too, a little tipsy, rested his head against the backrest, his eyes half closed, heard her groan, and turned his head to face her.

"I need to take a cab to my apartment, but it is hard to find one at this time." she said.

"Why don't you spend the night?" Layne suggested, his eyes half mast but questioning.

"Layne and I are sharing a room, but I can bunk with

Steve and Rex," Rami said with a smile. "Give you two some time alone."

This was definitely not what Juli had in mind at the beginning of the night, but she couldn't deny that she wanted to stay with Layne. Perhaps it was her low inhibitions because of the beer or that hot as hell moment at the venue, hiding in the shadows and reminding her of their chemistry, but she wanted more. She looked to Layne, who was now fully awake, eyes searching her gaze and waiting for her response. She nodded and the handsome smile that curled his lips nearly made her climb on top of him right there in the van. *What have you gotten yourself into?*

* * *

THEY WALKED INTO LAYNE, and Rami's room, and Juli took in the space. Walking over to the window, she glanced out at the street aglow with the colorful scones on the hotel, her mind a cacophony of waring thoughts. She could hear Rami rushing around on his side of the room, grabbing his things, and talking to Layne. The door closed, the sound of the latch echoing through the space and making her hyper aware that she and Layne were now alone. Before she could grapple with her thoughts again, warm arms came around her, his fingers sliding between hers, and she closed her eyes, resting her head back on his shoulder. She focused on breathing in and out slowly, trying to steady her heartbeat and temper the onslaught of emotions. Having him close was eliciting. His breath warmed her cheek and smelled sweet, like hops from the beer they enjoyed tonight as he whispered against her ear, "We don't have to do anything. I just want to hold you and have you in my arms."

"Okay." she managed, hot tears stinging her eyes as unexpected emotion hovered near the surface. She tried to blink away the threat of tears, but it was pointless. They escaped, trailing down her cheeks. She breathed deeply, exhaling in little tremors, her shoulders shaking with each hard breath. *Where was this coming from?* A tidal wave of emotion threatening to wash her away. She had waited so long to see him, to be with him and feel his presence surrounding her that the thought of that made all the pent-up emotions drown her.

He turned her around in his arms, his face as anguished as she felt, his cheeks wet and eyes glossy with tears. He leaned in and kissed her, a sob escaping against his lips, and he wrapped his arms around her protectively as she let out all she had been holding onto. Eight years of bottled-up anger, hurt, deep-seated animosity coming out like a flood against his chest. He rubbed her back tenderly, his hands threading through her hair, reassuring her it was okay to let these flood gates open. She wasn't sure how long they stood like that, her sobbing and him holding her close, but soon she found herself being led into the bathroom. He wet a washcloth with warm water and gently wiped her cheeks, removing the dark tracks left by her eye makeup and tears. She looked up at him, meeting his understanding gaze, and reached for his hand holding the cloth.

His brows furrowed slightly as she reached for the hem of her t-shirt and lifted it over her head. Reaching for the button on her leather pants, she looked towards the shower and asked, "Join me?"

He nodded, lifting his t-shirt over his head, and slipping it off. She rested her hand on his heart, feeling the rapid thump against her palm, and gazed up into his eyes, something so pure and profound passing between them. Removing the rest of their clothes, they both climbed into the shower, letting the warm water wash over their bodies. Although they were naked and vulnerable, there was nothing sexual about the moment. They washed each other lovingly, no words passing between them. Letting the water cleanse them of all the hurt and pain they had been holding onto, promising a clean slate.

CHAPTER 17

EIGHT YEARS AGO

April had arrived. The days were still cold and crisp, but the snow was all but gone from the spring rain. It had also been six months since Layne and Juli started dating, and he wanted to do something special for her.

"Is Juli staying for dinner on Saturday?" his mother asked as she set the dinner table. "If she is, I was thinking of making my black forest cake, which I know she loves so much."

"I want to take her out that night but thank you mama," he said, giving his mother's shoulder an appreciative squeeze.

"Is it a special occasion?" his father asked curiously as he took a seat at the head of the table.

"We've been dating for six months, so I want to plan a special date for her."

"Six months already. Time has gone by fast." His mother mused, taking a seat too. "How about you take her out for dinner, dress up a bit? Girls like it when you do something special like that."

"Worked for me," his father said, reaching for his mother's hand.

His parents had been married 41 years and were still very much in love with each other. Having that example in his life made him never doubt that he would someday find the same, and every time he considered the future, Juli's beautiful face was always there. Layne was aware it was crazy for him to think that way, considering their ages and the circumstances, but he did. He cared so deeply for her and was certain he was falling in love. An idea crossed his mind, and he looked up at his mother.

"Mama, do you know anyone here in town that makes jewellery, someone that could make something quickly for me?" he asked, knowing his mom knew everyone in town and loved to visit the local craft shows.

"Yes, I do. I will call her after dinner." She replied with a wink as Layne imagined Juli's beautiful face when he surprised her with his gift.

"Where are you taking me?" Juli asked as she watched the lights of St. Augustine come into view.

"Dinner and then I have a surprise," he replied, grinning ear to ear as he reached for her hand. She leaned in and gripped his bicep, while his heart thrummed wildly with her touch. He pulled into the parking lot of a colorful restaurant at one end of the small city and found a parking spot. Like a gentleman, he rounded his car and opened her door for her. Taking her hand, he looked up at the sign, her gaze following his.

"The Blue Corn." Juli said slowly, then, with a scrunched-up nose, turned to Layne. "What type of restaurant?"

"Mexican. Have you ever had it before?" he asked, curiously, as they made their way to the door.

"No, but I have heard of it. We have a few places in Hamburg." she replied. "But I have never been."

"I think you will love it. Rami's Abuela, or grandmother, owns this place."

Juli's eyes widened with excitement as they entered the restaurant. The colorful décor drawing them in as festive mariachi music played in the background. The smell of slow cooked meat, chili peppers and lime enveloped them, and Juli inhaled deeply.

"It smells so good," she said, squeezing his hand in approval.

"Oh, Layne, chico dulce!" a short stout silver haired woman exclaimed as she rushed over to them. Her eyes were a deep brown, and her smile was wide and welcoming as she gripped his face and kissed both of his cheeks with affection. Layne's face turned red, and Juli couldn't help but smile in amusement at this friendly woman greeting them. "And who is this beautiful girl with you? Is this your girlfriend I've heard so much about?"

This must be Rami's grandmother. Juli smiled down at her as she pulled Juli in for a hug too, squeezing her tightly. Releasing their embrace, she held her out at arm's length. "I'm everyone's Abuela and now I am yours too. Welcome to my restaurant."

Juli beamed down at the woman, instantly adoring her and feeling the warmth radiating off her tiny frame. Reaching for a couple of menus, she said, "C'mon kids, let me get you a special table."

Leading them to the back of the restaurant, she brought them to a small table in the corner. Layne pulled out Juli's chair and Abuela gave him a nod of approval as he took his seat across from her.

"Now, do you want menus, or do you want the Abuela special?" she asked with a twinkle in her eye and a wide smile.

The Abuela special was something she would do when they would come in with Rami, and it was always amazing. A little bit of everything.

"The Abuela special, please," he replied.

She took their drink orders and rushed off happily as Juli's gaze followed her. Juli's eyes roamed the space with wonder, taking in the colorful tablecloth and picado papel draping across on the ceiling. "It is all so colorful and pretty."

"Not as pretty as you," he replied, not skipping a beat as his eyes roamed over her floral knee length dress then back up to her face.

She sighed, her cheeks blooming with a rosy glow and in that moment, Layne was sure he had never seen anyone more beautiful.

"I have a gift for you," he said, eagerly reaching into his jacket pocket and pulling out a little box. The paper was a little rumpled, and his brows knit together as he tried to smooth it out.

"That is okay, Layne." she giggled, reaching out and stilling his hand. "I don't mind."

He shrugged with a little laugh and placed it in front of her. Picking it up, she unwrapped the paper to find a shiny gold box. Lifting the lid, her eyes widened as she pulled out a gold chain with an arrow pendant connecting both sides of the chain.

"It is so pretty, Layne." she whispered, her eyes as wide as saucers. "Can you help me put it on?" He rose from their table as she handed him the necklace and pulled her hair aside, allowing him to fasten it for her. His fingertips brushed the tender skin on the back of her neck, leaving goosebumps in their wake.

"An arrow?" she asked curiously, as she admired the pendant.

"So, you always know what direction you need to go," he said, the words coming out soft yet strangled, deep emotion edging his voice.

Surprised by the hint of melancholy in his voice, her eyes searched his, her brows furrowed in concern. "I will always find my way to you," she declared.

Repeating her words in his head, Layne tried to swallow down the emotion that rose in his throat, threatening to suffocate him. That her return to Hamburg at the end of summer was always looming. But now, sitting across from the most beautiful girl he had ever laid eyes on, knowing he was falling for her, the thought of not being able to see her was almost too much to bear. The reality of their impending goodbyes, smacking him right in the face. They could video chat, call and even text, but it wouldn't be the same as having her near, and the thought of not seeing her every day made his heart hurt. Pushing down the unexpected emotion, he leaned in and gave her a chaste kiss, the weight of the situation now a forethought in his mind.

* * *

AFTER DINNER, Layne drove them to a community park in the middle of the city. It was a place that carried a lot of fond memories for him growing up. On Sunday, after church, his parents would pack a lunch and take him there so he could play on the playground and get out his energy. They would go for long walks along the paved paths and climb the large hill overlooking the entire park.

"Can we go for a walk?" he asked. "It's chilly, but nice and clear tonight."

She nodded with a smile as she wrapped her colorful scarf around her neck and buttoned up her coat. Taking her hand, they walked down the lit walkway to a little bridge that covered a canal, allowing water to flow freely between two sides of a large pond. Her boots clicked on the wooden bridge and Layne stopped and pulled her into his chest. He held her close, inhaling the sweet smell of her spicy vanilla lotion, and sighed.

Juli sighed too and rested her head against the groove of his chest, neither wanting to let each other go. Silent emotion lingered thickly between them, as he grappled with what to say in this melancholy moment. He couldn't think of the words to adequately describe the way he felt about Juli. He wasn't sure if there were words to describe it. *Is this what falling in love is like? Those moments, even in silence, that you know you're with the only person you ever want to be with.*

Taking her hand, they walked together quietly around the loop of the pond and made their way towards the large hill in the middle of the park. Climbing it, they sat down on the grass. Juli nestled between his legs, her back to his front and his arms wrapped around her shoulders affectionately.

She leaned in and kissed his arm, then said so softly it was barely audible. "I love you, Layne."

Layne's pulse quickened as his heart jack hammered in his chest. *She loves me too!* he wanted to shout from the top of this hill. Hearing those words from her was overwhelming in the best possible way. He kissed her cheek and with profound emotion edging his voice, he declared, "I love you too, Juli. I love you very much."

She turned in his arms to face him, her eyes wide and brimming with tears as she added, "I am scared, Layne."

I'm scared too. This thing that was growing between them was so much more than a teenage crush or infatuation. It was very real to him, and he could see by the emotion on her face, it was very real for her, too.

He cupped her cheek, caressing the soft skin as he said, "I don't know what will happen after you go back to Germany, but I do know every day has been wonderful for me and I want to stay in touch."

She nodded, big fat tears escaping through her long lashes as she replied, "I want that too. But I can not imagine a day without you, Layne."

Layne's heart ached seeing that hopeless sadness in her

eyes, so he tried to deflect. "Let's not think of that yet. Let's just enjoy our time together, okay?"

She nodded and climbed onto his lap, straddling his hips. She brushed the hair back that always seemed to flop into his eyes and kissed him, long and hard, her tongue dipping into his mouth and tangling with his. His body began to heat and harden as she pushed him to the ground. His hands sliding up her thighs and over her hips, grazing the edge of her underwear as they devoured each other. He wasn't sure how long they kissed like that, but the realization that they were in a public park, and he could so easily take her right here right now, brought him back to reality, so he pulled his lips away from hers.

"Juli, we need to stop," he said, his voice rasping with each word. "I want you, but not like this, not out in the open for anyone to see."

As if the realization of what she was doing hit her too, she looked around to see a couple with a dog walking on the trail, and she turned her gaze back to his. "I just can not stop kissing you. I want to be with you, Layne." she confessed.

Sitting up, he wrapped his arms around her in a hug, kissing her hair affectionately. "Soon, Juli." he replied, knowing intimacy was something they both wanted. He didn't know when they would finally make that leap, but when they did, he was going to ensure their first time was special and worthy of the growing love between them.

CHAPTER 18

Waking with Juli's warm body curled around him felt like a dream. Like a perfect dream that ran on repeat in his head over the past eight years. Burying his face in her soft hair, he inhaled deeply the smell of her combined with his body wash. She stirred, her long lashes fluttering, but she didn't wake, so he pulled her closer and let out a long-contented exhale. Last night was a breakthrough for them. When she pulled him into the shower with her, he wanted nothing more than to reacquaint himself with her beautiful body, but that wasn't what she needed at that moment. He needed to take care of her, show her he still cherished her, that he was here, supporting her, and that he would not walk away from her again. They needed that cleansing ritual so they could wash away every last remnant of lingering pain before they could move forward with their relationship. After their shower, he dressed her in one of his t-shirts and tucked her into bed. He watched her a while, stroking her hair affectionately as she eventually gave into sleep. Then he climbed in next to her, curling himself around her body encased in her warmth as he followed her to dreamland.

Her eyes fluttered open and met his gaze as he leaned in and kissed her forehead. "Good morning," he whispered, trailing his fingertips across her cheek and over her ear. He remembered how much she liked that, and she sighed, instantly melting in his arms. "I think it's afternoon, actually, but I hope you slept well."

"I did," she replied groggily as she peeled her body from his and rolled off the bed. Watching her as she strode towards the bathroom, his t-shirt just covering the swell of her behind, his body instantly hardened at the sight of her. Juli was tall, and curvy in all the right places and he remembered like yesterday how those curves felt in his hands. She returned a few minutes later and leaned in kissing him softly, her breath smelling like mint. Although the clock was ticking on their time together and he wanted to be intimate with her, more than anything, he wasn't going to push it, letting her decide how far they would take this.

"Sorry, give me a few minutes too," he said, knowing he needed to calm his body down.

Climbing out of bed, he groaned, unable to hide the effect she was having on him as he caught her coy smile. Disappearing behind the partition, he exhaled and closed the bathroom door. Gripping the sink, he glanced up at his reflection in the mirror. His hair was completely askew, and he had dark circles under his eyes. Yet, despite his disheveled appearance, he couldn't help but let a smile tug at his lips. Juli was here with him, just the two of them, and he was being given a second chance to make it right. *She is letting you in.*

With that thought repeating in his head, he quickly took care of his morning needs and strode out of the bathroom, rounding the corner of the partition, and stopped in his tracks. There, laid out on the covers, was Juli, completely naked, her big brown eyes locked on his. His breath caught as his eyes journeyed over every inch of her creamy skin on full display just for him. *Just as beautiful as I remembered her.* The desire to touch her, taste her, consume her overtook him. His body hardened as he looked, his fill meeting her wanton gaze.

"Layne." she murmured, her voice husky and needy. Striding over to the bed, he curled his fingers around the waistband of his briefs and slid them off. Her eyes unabashedly reacquainting with his ample length, she sucked in a breath as her gaze slowly drifted back to his and she smiled coquettishly.

"Make me feel good, strong man." She purred, her past term of endearment for him getting a little upgrade. "I need you."

He crawled onto the bed; her legs falling open to him as he took in the rosy softness of her glistening sex. He halted, his eyes meeting hers so hazy with need and desire. "I need to taste you, before I make love to you," he said as he lowered himself and lifted her core to his waiting mouth. Taking one long lap through her silky folds, her breath caught as her back arched off the bed and she moaned out with pleasure. Teasing and toying with her body, he circled the sweet spot he knew would make her lose control. He had dreamt of this with her, taking control of her pleasure as her body trembled under each long indulgent lap of his tongue. He would wake up each time, salivating at the thought and wondering if he would someday get the chance. All the times they had been together, two teens young and inexperienced, he did not know how to elicit her pleasure like this. Now, as an adult, he knew exactly what he needed to do to make her feel good and to make her moan his name. Her hands found his hair, coiling through his locks as he devoured the sweetness of her core. She gripped the strands almost painfully as he lavished attention where she pulsed and ached until she gasped and shuddered, cresting on his lips. As she came down from her release, he crawled over her, hovering above her with a sexy, satisfied smile.

She opened her eyes and met his gaze, still dark with desire. "You have never done that to me before." She said, her hands running over the taut muscles of his shoulders and down his back. "I liked it." Capturing her mouth in an erotic kiss, the sweetness of her, still on his lips, his tongue slid with hers, making her purr against his mouth. Pulling his lips away, still sharing a breath, his eyes met hers, dark with desire. "I need to be inside you," he breathed out; his body poised at her entrance. "I need to feel you again."

"Please." she begged, as she gripped his behind and he pressed forward, savoring the exquisite tightness as he entered her. As their bodies fused to one, the memory of their first time returned to his consciousness. He was so scared he would hurt her and took his time allowing her body to adjust to him. Now, all these years later, her body opened like a flower, taking him in fully, her hips seeking and accepting all he had to offer. He kissed her, slow sensual kisses as delicious as each grind and press of their coupled bodies. They found a rhythm so perfect; it made all his senses heighten. The softness of her skin against the hard edges of his own, the pulsing squeeze of her core surrounding him, the sweet sounds she made with each push and pull. He wanted to stop time and memorize, each second, having never had anything feel more euphoric, than this moment with the two of them connected in the most intimate way possible. Feeling the slow burn low on his spine, he rocked into her molten heat and quickened his pace. As his body, prepared to give into the pleasure, the feelings he had tried unsuccessfully to bury for the past eight years, rose to the surface in a rush. *I need to tell her. She needs to know.*

"Juli, I love you," he confessed. "I never stopped. I never will."

Her eyes shone with tears as she gripped his hair, bringing his lips crashing to hers, kissing him deeply, breathlessly. She inhaled sharply against his lips and cried his name into his mouth as her orgasm overtook her, her inner muscles gripping him tightly. With eyes locked on each other and staccato breaths, he followed. The sweet burn ignited into a wildfire as he let go deep inside her warm, willing body. Covering her to cradle her body with his own, they trembled with aftershocks, trying to catch their breaths as she whispered the words he so longed to hear, "I love you too."

CHAPTER 19

EIGHT YEARS AGO

Primrose High School was bustling with activity. With the Spring Musical complete and final exams a week away, graduation was the hot topic of conversation, especially who was going to be named the class valedictorian. Although the senior class only consisted of 30 kids, never did Layne expect to be in the running for this role. Then, when he found out, he was nominated and the subsequent vote ruled in his favor, he was sure it had to do with his newfound popularity as Juli's boyfriend. Either way, he was now responsible for coming up with a speech for graduation.

Finally, the day arrived, and Layne was a little nervous. Not about the graduation, not about his speech, but because tonight was going to be the night. After graduation, after the dinner, rather than attending the all-night safe grad party at a local reception hall, he had booked them a room at a hotel in Winnipeg. With their alibis in place and a mutual agreement between the two of them, they were both eager to take their relationship to the next level.

Layne slipped a small duffle bag into the trunk of his car and quickly closed it as his mom and Dad exited the house. He smiled at them as they walked over to his car and his mom handed him the corsage he had ordered for Juli. His mom already had tears in her eyes as she pulled him in for a hug. "I am so proud of you Layne." she cooed as she let go of their embrace and looked up into his face. "Are you ready for your speech?"

"I think so," he said, patting the inside pocket of his tailored jacket that held the paper he had written it on.

"You go pick up Juli and we'll meet you at the church." His father said with a smile as he clapped him on the back.

Nodding, he took the corsage his mother held and slipped into his car, peeling out of the driveway towards town.

Five minutes later, he arrived at the Parkers and pulled down his visor mirror to check out his reflection. Straightening his burgundy tie, he flipped the visor up and got out of his car, corsage in hand. Smoothing down his navy jacket and wiping his sweaty palms on his tailored pants, he strode towards the door.

Mrs. Parker greeted him with her usual bright smile. "Layne, happy graduation! Don't you look handsome." She commented, giving him a once over. "Come in. Juli will be out shortly."

Layne walked into their front entrance. Mr. Parker, Mrs. Parker and Juli's exchange partner Lisa all smiles as they waited quietly and awkwardly for Juli to make her appearance. Rocking on the heels of his shiny dress shoes, he stuffed his hands in his pockets. They were a nice family, but he was always a little uncomfortable with their need to be so formal.

"Ah, here she is!" Mrs. Parker exclaimed as Juli floated down the hallway, a vision in cascading burgundy.

His eyes widened and jaw slacked as he saw the most beautiful girl in the world come towards him. Her dress was long and flowing, almost sweeping the floor with a bodice of intricate lace, spaghetti straps, and a sweetheart neckline that just teased the tops of her breasts. The dress was, all things considered, appropriate for a girl of 16, but when she walked towards him, her long silky leg peeked out of a thigh high slit on the side. His mouth went dry, and he knew he was gawking, but he didn't care. She was a vision, and she was his girlfriend.

Before Layne could even formulate words, Mrs. Parker leaned in and gave Juli a hug. "You look beautiful Juli."

She gave her a look of thanks and turned to Layne, her large brown eyes sparkling playfully at him as a knowing smile tugged at her perfectly glossed lips.

Layne held out the corsage to her, and she took it, her eyes turning dreamy at his gift. Helping her open the clamshell, he slipped it on her wrist as Mrs. Parker took pictures and gushed at what a beautiful couple they were. Mrs. Parker made them go outside and pose for a few more photos in front of the large evergreen in the front yard. Normally, Layne loathed this kind of attention, but with his arm around Juli's waist, the swirl of her intoxicating spicy vanilla lotion surrounding him, and her softness pressed against the side of his body he wasn't about to complain about a few harmless pictures. Juli glanced up at him, a coy look on her face as they prepared to leave, and she slipped inside the house to retrieve her backpack, explaining that she wanted to take a change of clothes for the all-night party. Layne's eyes flitted to Juli with her little white lie, and she gave him a sly look of reassurance that they had no idea about their plans. Waving goodbye to the Parkers, Layne reached for Juli's hand, lacing his fingers with hers as they drove to the church. Giving her the full gentleman treatment, he opened her door for her and took her hand to help her out of his car.

She gazed up at him through her impossibly long lashes and smiled lovingly. That look doing crazy things to both his body and his heart.

"Sorry, I was speechless when I first saw you," he apologized, holding her close. "You're beautiful, just so incredibly beautiful." He said, leaning in and planting a soft kiss on her lips.

Pulling away, she let out a little giggle as she wiped away some of her burgundy lipstick from his mouth. She took in his sharply tailored suit and wrapped her arms around him, looking deep into his eyes. "And you are the handsomest boyfriend ever."

"I love you," he said, his fingertips tracing the line of her necklace and down to the arrow pendant resting at the hollow of her throat. He smoothed it with this thumb and smiled.

"I love you too," she whispered. Both beaming with hearts in their eyes as he took her hand, leading her across the parking lot into the building.

* * *

AS WAS TRADITION IN PRIMROSE, the graduation ceremony was always held at a church that was situated on the highway just outside of town. This church was large and expansive and had a huge sanctuary that could accommodate all the friends, family and even some curious onlookers from town to the ceremony.

With Juli seated with his family and Layne, now dressed in his cap and gown, he looked around at his classmates, many of whom he had known since kindergarten. They were smiling, laughing, some were hugging and crying. All people he had a history with, in some way. The finality of it all hit him in that moment and the importance of his speech became clear. Although he had a rough speech written, as he looked around at all the familiar faces of students and staff, he knew at that moment exactly what he wanted to say.

The piano music started, and the class lined up in alphabetical order. Entering the sanctuary, following the caravan of graduates down the middle aisle, Layne spotted Juli radiating pure joy from the second row next to his mother. He couldn't take his eyes off her as he walked and almost stumbled into the classmate in front of him. Shaking his head at his clumsiness, he climbed the stairs and took a seat at the front, next to the principal, the spot designated for the valedictorian. The ceremony was a combination of school and municipality speeches, scholarships, and awards and finally the time had come for his valedictory speech. He rose from his seat, all eyes in the sanctuary on him, everyone waiting with bated breath, as he stepped to the podium. He fished out the paper he stuffed into his pocket and pulled it out, making a show of unfolding the paper and holding it out in front of him. He looked up at the audience and, with a playful smile, ripped it in half and let it fall. Several of his classmates, as well as the audience watching, either chuckled or gasped as he leaned into the microphone.

"Hello everyone, I'm Layne Stark, your 2015 Class Valedictorian." one of his classmates let out a loud 'woo hoo', eliciting smiles and giggles from the onlookers. "I'm also that quiet guy in the back of every classroom who would much rather be playing bass guitar in his garage with his band than be at school each day." He glanced at the principal, whose brows were now furrowed, and Layne shrugged as he turned his attention back to the audience. "However, this year was different for me. Yes, I probably would still rather be making music than studying, but this year, I met someone very special who helped me come out of my shell, my girlfriend, Juli Roth." he said, glancing down at Juli's impossibly pretty face that was now riveted to his words. "Anyone who meets Juli knows she has this joyful spirit that fills every room. She floats around the school, talking with everyone, making friends with whomever she meets and truly enjoys being a part of Primrose High School and our quiet small town. As I watched her truly appreciate her time here, I started to open my eyes and truly see everyone else around me as well. I saw my classmates, who are all a bunch of fun, weird, interesting, and intelligent human beings. Human beings that have the potential to do great and remarkable things in this world. I saw my teachers as not just the unholy providers of endless hours of homework, but as people who truly care about us and are invested in our future success. I saw our school and this amazing community of Primrose as something to be truly grateful for. It is you, our families, our friends, our school, and our community that got us here. We are one big loving, sometimes dysfunctional family and I know, I for one am proud to be a part of it. So, on behalf of myself and the rest of my class, thank you. Thank you for believing in us, thank you for pushing us and thank you for molding us into the best versions of ourselves as we look towards our bright and beautiful futures."

He stepped away from the podium, taking the pieces of his speech with him as the entire room erupted with cheers, and everyone got to their feet, giving him a standing ovation. Layne returned to his seat, his classmates slapping him on his back as he took his place. He glanced down at his mom, who was dabbing her eyes with a tissue, his dad whose chin was up, prouder than he had ever seen and his eyes drifted to Juli, the girl who made his final year of school one he would never forget.

CHAPTER 20

The desire to show Layne her home city and the human need for sustenance drew them from his bed. Picking up coffees and croissants from the cafe down the street from the hotel, they made their way to the closest U-Bahn station so Juli could make a quick stop at home to change her clothes. They walked down the cobblestone street till they came to a four floor U shaped apartment complex with a nicely landscaped garden in the middle. The building was a classic bright red brick and although it was old, looked clean and well maintained. They entered the entrance and climbed two flights of stairs until they arrived on the third floor. She guided him down a long, bright hallway and stopped at a blue door.

"This is me," she said with a smile as she unlocked her apartment. He entered and smiled, feeling the warmth of being surrounded by Juli and all the things she treasured. The small, narrow living room had large windows at the end and a comfy looking blue couch with a TV against the opposite wall on a white stand. A tall bookshelf filled with books, knickknacks, and pictures stood off to the side, and a little two-person white table with matching chairs was pushed up against a blue wall in the same color as her front door.

"Would you like a tour?" she asked, setting her purse and keys on the table. "I promise, it will not take long," she said with a giggle. "This is my living room." She said, holding out her arms in the room they were standing before she walked into a narrow galley-style kitchen with all the cabinets along one wall and painted in the same blue from the living room. "This is my kitchen."

"You have a balcony," he said, walking over to the door at the end of the kitchen and peeking out onto a small brick balcony. A little bistro set was set in the corner.

"When it is warmer, I like to sit out there and read." She said with a smile as she closed the door, and they strode into the last room. "And this is my bedroom." She said, her arms wide as she turned in the space. In the middle was a low-profile European style bed with a bright blue and yellow comforter that was flagged by two end tables. In the corner was a simple desk with her laptop, a bookshelf on the far wall, and a series of hooks with different scarves hung like a colorful piece of art across from the bed. A long narrow window brought in natural light, and it was spacious and airy despite the small apartment.

"This place feels like you," he said with a smile as he took it all in.

"Thank you. I moved in here after my mother died. We lived on the other side of the building in a larger apartment at the time, so when it was just me, this smaller apartment felt not so empty." Opening her closet, she rummaged inside, pulling out a pair of jeans and a soft green sweater. He took a seat on the bed, leaning back on his elbows as he watched her move around her space. When they were together, he often found himself just watching her. She always moved with such confidence when they were younger. With a confidence beyond her years. Now, as a grown woman, you could see she simply knew who she was and didn't seem to concern herself with what others thought of her. That effortless confidence was one thing that he found wildly attractive.

"You always look at me like a hungry wolf," she commented with a laugh as she picked out a scarf and wrapped it around her neck.

"I just enjoy admiring you," he said as she pulled out a pair of boots from the closet. "And you are incredibly sexy."

Juli turned, abandoning her boots as she stalked over to him, and pushing him back on her bed. Climbing over his body to straddle his hips, she leaned down and kissed him passionately, the smoldering embers between them igniting into a fire. Just as Layne was about to slide his hand under her sweater, she pulled her lips away and crawled off him, giving him a teasing grin. "More of that later, but for now, I want to show you my city."

CHAPTER 21

EIGHT YEARS AGO

With his diploma in hand, countless photos taken, along with what felt like a million hugs and congratulations, the crowd was finally thinning out, so Layne saw his chance to steal a moment with Juli. He grabbed her hand, pulling her to the side of the building, in the shadows, out of the view of everyone still there. She gazed up at him, looping her arms around his neck, and he lowered his lips to hers for a searing kiss. His hunger for her was palpable. Their tongues slid together as a sensual preview of what this night had in store. His fingers found the slit of her dress as he ran his hand up her smooth leg and pressed her into the wall. His hand disappeared under her skirt, teasing the edge of her underwear, and a moan escaped her lips. "I want you so much." He confessed between lavish, needy kisses.

"I want you too," she replied, pulling her lips from his breathless as she rested her hand on his chest. "Soon."

He groaned and leaned in, touching his forehead to

hers as he asked, "Can't we ditch the dinner and go right to the hotel?"

She giggled and pushed him away from her playfully, making him stumble back with a smile. "I am sure your parents will notice if we are not there."

Juli was right. They had worked so hard to craft their alibis that if they disappeared now, everyone would know. This night was something between them and no one else. Neither Layne nor Juli had shared their plans with anyone. Not his bandmates, and not even Juli's friends were aware of their plans. This night was all about them.

Throughout the dinner, Layne couldn't keep his hands off Juli. Under the table his hand kept finding the slit of her dress and he couldn't help caressing her leg, his fingers finding the sensitive skin of her inner thighs. Juli luckily found it amusing and did her own bit of teasing, tugging at his hair, and trailing her fingernails along the back of his neck whenever she had the chance. It was driving him crazy and once the dinner was done and they said their goodbyes to his family, he couldn't get to his car fast enough.

"Are you excited?" Juli asked as they reached the city limits of Winnipeg. "You are driving so fast."

"Sorry..." he answered, easing off the accelerator. "Just eager, I guess."

Juli smiled, curling her fingers around his bicep and staring at him dreamily, the heat of her hand making his body hum with anticipation. They had dated eight months, and he had been patient, letting her decide when the time was right to take this next step. He could surely wait just a little longer to be together. He needed this time to get himself together and tamp down the nervousness settling in his belly. It's just every time he glanced over at her and she'd flash him that knowing smile. His body would flame, and his mind would drift to everything he wanted to experience with her.

They pulled into the parking lot of a large hotel on the edge of the city, and he retrieved their bags from the trunk as he took her hand, and they entered the hotel. Handing the concierge his ID, he looked at it, scrutinizing him for a few moments, then passed it back to him. Layne knew he was checking his age and made an exception with him being almost 18. Layne internally exhaled as he checked them in, grateful their plans were not being derailed.

"Alright, Mr. Stark, just take this elevator," the concierge informed, pointing to shiny elevator doors. "Go up to the 7th floor and your room is at the end of the hallway." He handed him the keycards, and they made their way into the elevator.

Juli reached for his hand, threading her fingers with his, and he could feel the air between them swirl with a combination of lust, anticipation and nervousness. Glancing at her, his eyes softened as he watched her stare unblinking at the floor numbers going up, her breaths shallow and tense. "Are you nervous?" he asked, knowing the answer before he asked it.

Her eyes flitted to meet him, as she answered his question honestly. "I am a little."

He pulled her into him, his brows drawing together as he searched her eyes. "We don't have to do anything if you don't want to. I'm okay if you aren't ready."

She shook her head vigorously. "No, I am ready. It's just I don't know what I am doing exactly. I mean, I know, but I do not." She buried her head in his chest and giggled. The sound of her melodic laugh cutting through their nervous tension and going straight to his heart.

He lifted her chin to look straight into her eyes as he admitted, "I don't know either, Juli. But together we'll figure it out." Then he lowered his lips to hers for a gentle kiss.

The elevator dinged, breaking their embrace, and they walked hand in hand down the hall, finding their room. Layne pulled out the key card, and the door opened for them. Their room was spacious and modern, with two queen beds, a TV mounted on the wall, a desk in the corner, and a chair by the large window. Juli entered first, glancing into the bathroom and striding over to the chair, setting down her backpack. Her heartbeat wildly in her chest, and her skin heated as she mentally tried to calm herself down. Pulling back the curtain, she looked down on the quieter side street below. This place was nice, and Layne had chosen well. She turned to see Layne watching her as he set down his keys on the desk and removed his wallet from his pants pocket. Their hesitant gazes met, his brown eyes piercing hers, and her heart skipped a beat. *I love him so much. Tonight, I will give him all of me.*

He slowly approached her, his hands settling on her hips as they looked deep into each other's eyes. A sweet smile tugged at his lips, and he lowered his head to plant a feather-like kiss on her lips, making her melt into his arms. *He is so wonderful.* Burying her head in his chest, he wrapped his strong arms around her. Feeling his rapid heartbeat against her cheek, she swallowed nervously and glanced up at him through her long lashes. "I am going to get changed," she said softly, a rosy flush heating her cheeks with her words. He nodded, letting her go and stepping aside to let her grab her backpack. Backpack in hand, she rushed past him, slipping into the bathroom.

The bathroom door closed. She rested her back against the door, letting the smooth cool surface temper her heated body. Closing her eyes and inhaling deeply, letting a calming breath out. *You need to calm down, Juli. You have waited, and he has been patient.* Layne had been so patient. He had never pressured her and had never done anything that made her feel uncomfortable. He always let her take the lead, and she had no doubt he would do the same tonight. *Then why are you freaking out?*

Closing her eyes, she took in another cleansing breath, trying to calm her heart. She smiled, thinking of the past year and all her stolen moments with Layne. Moments she would never forget, and tonight was just another one of those precious moments. Pushing off the door she unzipped her backpack and pulled out her toiletry bag. She took out her toothbrush and started brushing her teeth, trying to ease the anticipation and nervousness vibrating through her body. Slipping out of her dress, she hung it on the hook behind the door and put on the satiny camisole with matching pajama shorts she found on a shopping trip with Harlow. Surveying her reflection in the mirror, she touched the shiny material, trailing her finger tips over the lace on the neckline, feeling pretty, and wondering if Layne would like it. *Will he think I'm sexy?* Letting out a nervous giggle, a flush of heat settled in her cheeks again. She went to work washing her face and brushing her hair and as she was zipping her toiletry bag back up, she saw the condoms at the bottom of her bag. Condoms she had purchased on a rare solo trip into the drugstore while Mrs. Parker waited in the car. She opened the box, pulled one out and looked at it, wondering if Layne knew how to put it on. The thought of that made the heat surge through her body and settle in her core. Taking a few more cleansing breaths, she took one more look at her reflection. *You are ready.*

Exiting the bathroom, her breath caught as she took in the romantic scene. On every possible surface sat tiny battery powered tea lights illuminating the room in an ethereal glow. Hand on her heart, her eyes found Layne's across the room as he sat patiently on the bed. He rose, dressed only in his boxer briefs, his face and lean body illuminated by the sea of little lights. *He is so beautiful.* Taking her in with reverence, his eyes twinkling with the flickers of light, his gaze slowly drifting back up to meet hers.

"I love you, Juli." he declared on a breath, love and desire pooling in his eyes.

In that perfect moment, the power of their feelings surrounded them. Tears of unbridled love brimmed in her eyes and need to touch him and share this sacred moment settled low in her belly. With a rapidly beating heart, and an all-consuming passion, she bridged the gap, unable to stop the tidal wave of love and lust from drowning them both as their lips crashed together and they tumbled to the bed.

CHAPTER 22

PRESENT DAY

Hand in hand, Juli and Layne toured Hamburg, Juli bringing him to all her favorite places in the city. Hopping on and off the U-Bahn, she brought him to the Rathausmarkt. They dipped in and out of shops on Jungfernstieg and she took him to her favorite park in the entire city, Alsterpark. Although it was cold and the Fall chill bit at their faces, they sat on a bench wrapped around each other as they watched the boats on the Alster River with the Hamburg Skyline as a backdrop.

"I really like it here." Layne said, pulling Juli tighter into his warmth.

"It is much prettier in the springtime when the cherry trees blossom." She replied, glancing towards the trees that lined the walkway. "In Spring these trees are full of delicate pink flowers, and they smell amazing."

He buried his nose in her neck and inhaled deeply. "As amazing as you smell?" he asked.

Juli giggled and sighed as she gripped his bicep and

rested her head on his shoulder. "I love being here with you," she said, raising her head to meet his eyes. "I love you Layne, so very much."

He reached over and caressed her cheek tenderly. "I love you too," he replied as he leaned in and kissed her gently, the softness of his lips making emotion rise in her chest. *God, I love him so much. I have always loved him. There has never been anyone else for me.* Memories of their year together flowing like the river before them. All those stolen moments they spent talking, laughing, kissing. How they would check in with each other throughout the day. All the dinners with his family and fun with his friends. He had given her such a wonderful gift that year. Coming to Canada was her first experience abroad and on that first day of school, she was admittedly scared and kind of lost. She had a hard time understanding people, her thoughts always going to German, and everything was so different from the city school she was used to. A true culture shock. Then she met this handsome boy, sitting alone at the back of the class, that could understand her broken English and made her feel welcome. Layne had been her safe harbour throughout that year, a place where she always felt at home. *Layne feels like home to you.* That thought, making her think about what she wanted.

She gazed off into the distance, taking in the cityscape as her mind went into overdrive with questions. *Could I ever leave Hamburg? Could I leave my country? Could I make a life with Layne?* The idea of moving on and starting over completely was appealing in many ways, especially with her mother gone and no family close. But what would she do if she followed him? Certainly, there were not a lot of entertainment journalists in Primrose. There likely were no journalists at all. Maybe she could write. Write that legendary novel she always dreamt of publishing. She had no definite answers, and yet she was certain, deep down in her soul, that their story would not end after this weekend.

CHAPTER 23

EIGHT YEARS AGO

*L*ayne's eyes opened hesitantly, adjusting his eyes as beams of sunlight peeked through the curtains reflecting on the wall. The room was quiet, a peaceful early summer morning as he held Juli's warm body close to his, her soft hair fanned out on the pillow like a halo. Like the angel she was. His hand was splayed on her bare stomach, so soft and supple under his touch. He had never lain with a girl like this. Their naked bodies curled around each other like two pieces of a puzzle. It was the most content he had ever felt. His mind drifted to last night, finally consummating their relationship. Everything about it was sacred and special. Was it perfect? Probably not. But was it perfect for them? Yes, most definitely. Both nervous and completely inexperienced, they figured it out and when they both found their pleasure; it was truly magical. *My beautiful Juli. I love her so much; I want to spend every night with her like this. Wrapped in each other's arms.* It was a foolish thought, considering the reality of what they were facing. Their time together was far too quickly fading away. *Will I see her after she returns in August? Will we be able to stay together and figure out how to make a long-distance relationship work? Do long-distance relationships even work at all? Especially ones with an entire ocean between them.* All these thoughts and questions ran through his mind on a loop. The only thing he knew for sure in that moment was that he loved her and always would. She was his love of a lifetime; of that, he was certain. *But will that lifetime be together?* That, he didn't know.

She stirred, her body seeking him. He pulled her closer, the thrill of being able to hold and touch her like this beyond surreal. He trailed his fingers along her hip and down her leg, making her shiver and let out a little giggle. He loved her melodic laugh and started tickling her sides, making her squirm and squeal with delight.

"Layne!" she exclaimed as he relented and pulled her into him again, resting his chin on her shoulder and burying his face in her hair. She sighed contentedly, "This is so nice, just you and me like this."

"I wish we could lie like this forever," he confessed. "That you would never have to go back, and we just continue to be us, always."

He surprised himself with his words. Words he was thinking but would not say aloud. Something he wasn't wanting to put out there, at least not yet.

She turned in his arms, her big brown eyes searching his, "I must go back, Layne. I have no choice. Hamburg is my home."

"Can't I be your home?" he asked, knowing the question was selfish and absurd as emotion rose high in his throat and he swallowed it down painfully.

She brushed his hair from his eyes, her eyes welling up with tears. He didn't mean to make her cry with his question, and he didn't want to hear her say she needed to go home again. Not now, not after the wonderful night they shared with each other. Before she could speak, he captured her lips in a long deep kiss. That stifled any words she may want to say. She melted into him, their bodies fitting together seamlessly. The desire to make love to his girlfriend surged through his body. He needed to distract her, distract himself, suspend time and deflect any thoughts of their impending goodbyes. This moment right now with her in his arms, the only thing that mattered.

RETURNING from their blissful love bubble and with summer break underway, Layne had two priorities that summer, Juli, and his band. Having crossed the barrier of intimacy, Layne and Juli couldn't keep their hands off each other. Any chance they got to have sex, they took it, and it didn't matter where it was. It was like a faucet had been turned on, and there was no way to shut it off. His car, the garage, even at home with his parents' upstairs. They were wild for each other. Completely reckless and wild.

Layne watched from the window as Mrs. Parker drove off the driveway and Juli made her way up the walkway to the front door. He opened the door, expecting her big bright eyes and huge smile to greet him, but all he got was a half smile; her usual twinkling eyes were flat, and his brows furrowed in concern.

"Juli, sweetheart! Wie geht es dir?" his mother greeted her as she always did, wanting to know how she was doing.

"I am good, Mrs. Stark, thank you. Here to watch a movie with Layne." she said, feigning a sweet smile as she gripped tightly to her backpack.

Layne surveyed her, seeing her smile was strained, and that something was wrong. He took her hand and led her downstairs to his bedroom, closing the door behind him. Immediately, she flopped down on his bed, let out a trembling breath and covered her eyes with her hands.

"What's wrong?" he asked, taking a seat next to her and putting his hand on her thigh. "Talk to me, Juli."

She removed her hands and flopped them over her head, turning her head to meet his gaze. "I think I'm pregnant."

Pregnant? Layne could feel the color drain from his face. He leaned forward, resting his elbows on his legs as he ran his hands through his hair and stood up, pacing the length of his room, her words now on repeat in his head. She sat up and watched him, her big, beautiful eyes welling up. Seeing her tears, he stopped and asked, "Are you sure?"

"I am late, Layne. A whole week. I am never late; it always happens when it is supposed to." She replied, concern etched on her face.

He sat down on the bed next to her and took her hand

in his, lacing their fingers together. "Have you taken a test yet?"

"I have one in my backpack. I asked to go to the drugstore telling Mrs. Parker I needed supplies for, you know, and bought one." She explained as she met Layne's concerned eyes with her own. "I am scared to find out."

He squeezed her hand, the reality of the situation slowly catching up with him. She was going back to Germany in five weeks. Leaving here with no definitive plans to come back. They had used protection every single time without fail. How was this even possible?

Reaching over, he touched her face with affection and wiped a tear sliding down her cheek. "Whatever happens, we'll figure this out together, okay?"

She got up from the bed. Now it was her turn to pace. "I leave for home soon. What happens if I am pregnant? I am alone across an ocean with a baby, and I am just a teenager. I have two more years of school. How will I have a baby and go to school?"

This situation was messed up any way you looked at it. Juli had no choice but to go back to Hamburg. That was where her life was, her school, her family, and her friends. Then, if she was indeed pregnant, where did that leave him? His child and the girl he loved were across an ocean. His head ached painfully as worry took over. *How will I see her? How will I see them?* He flopped back on the bed and closed his eyes, wishing he wasn't here having these thoughts. These desperate, hollow thoughts about the future. Then it occurred to him, *I am done with school. I have choices. I don't need to be tied to Primrose.* He got up suddenly, his eyes meeting Juli's. "I will move to

Germany. I will quit the band, pack up my things and go with you."

A laugh escaped Juli's mouth, and she looked at him like he had lost his mind. "You can not do that, Layne. Your life is here, in Primrose. Your parents would be devastated and your band...you can not break up the band."

"But I would, I would leave everything to be with you and our..." he looked down at her stomach. "...baby."

"If there is a baby," she volleyed.

"Let's find out, then." He said, reaching for her backpack that she had set on the floor and handing it to her.

She fished through her backpack and pulled out the box, handing it to him. "Can you tell me what to do? My English is good, but I don't know if I will understand everything."

He nodded, opening the box, and handing her the test, then opening the instructions explaining to her how to take it. She slipped into his bathroom and emerged a minute later holding the stick. They returned to his room, and he closed the door, setting it on his desk as their eyes locked on the test.

"How long do we wait?" she asked.

"A few minutes."

They watched as one horizontal line showed quickly and a very faint vertical line appeared afterwards. Juli picked up the test and squinted at it, bringing her gaze to Layne, who was looking at the instructions again.

"It says if you have a plus sign, it is positive," he said, taking the test from her hands and looking at it closely. "It is light, but it's there."

Juli's face turned white as she slowly walked over to his bed and sat down, resting her head in her hands. "I can not be pregnant; I don't want that yet," she whispered hoarsely, as she looked up, meeting his eyes. "I want to be a mother someday, but not now. Not like this."

His throat constricted painfully at the fear edging her voice and he sat down next to her, pulling her into an embrace, holding her protectively to his chest as she cried. He wasn't ready for this either, but they had no other choice. They were going to be parents, whether they were ready or not.

PRESENT DAY

The lights of the city were bright against the cobblestones as they made their way back to Juli's apartment. Having made a stop at the hotel, Layne let his bandmates know he was spending the next two nights with Juli and would meet them at the train station on Monday morning. When they got to her house, he rolled his suitcase into her bedroom, finding a place against the wall.

"I need a shower." Juli said, walking into her room, with her scarf in her hand and hanging it on the hook. "Will you shower with me?" she asked, lifting her sweater over her head and unbuttoning the button of her jeans. His eyes darkened as he took in her large breasts barely contained by her modest cotton bra. She slipped off her jeans, tossing them into a basket in the corner, and reached behind her back to unfasten her bra. Sliding it down her arms, she tossed it with her jeans and sweater and stood before him in just her cotton underwear with her hands on her hips. He hadn't moved, his eyes roaming over all the dips and swells of her body. Juli was very aware that Layne liked all her curves; he liked them back then and she could see he liked them right now. Over the years, she had filled out more, trading in the soft subtle barely developed curves for an enviable hourglass figure. "Well…" she started a smile tugging at her lips. "…will you be joining me in the shower?" she asked, curling her fingers into the waistband of her underwear and sliding them down her long legs and tossing them in the basket.

"Yeah." he replied as if broken from his trance. "You are just so gorgeous; I can't take my eyes off you."

She giggled, rolled her eyes, and strode towards him as he started to undress. "How about you come with me, strong man, and I will let you touch me instead of just looking?"

With her tease, Layne quickly removed his clothes, falling to the bed as he tried to remove his jeans with lightning speed. Juli giggled and shook her head at his eagerness as she strode towards her bathroom, giving him a little extra sway of her behind as she went. Before she could even get into the shower, Layne was there, his large warm hands on her waist as she led them into the walk-in shower. Adjusting the temperature to warm, she turned around to be met with Layne's lustful gaze. She had already had the opportunity to see him, in all his naked glory, but now, with the steam of the shower making his skin glisten, she could truly admire the man he had become. Once this tall, lean boy, now a toned, defined man. His shoulders and arms showed just the right amount of muscle, obviously from carrying around equipment for years. His pectorals were defined but not huge and his stomach was taut and toned, with just a tease of a six-pack. Then there was the rest of him, just the thought of gripping his firm behind as he pumped into her and the feel of his hardness deep inside her body, making her core beg to have him inside her again. Ridiculously aroused at the thought, she pushed him against the far wall of the shower, the spray barely hitting them as she grabbed his face and kissed him hungrily, every curve of her body pressing him against the cool hard tile. Suddenly he reversed their position, taking control, her back now to the corner. Caging her in, he kissed her, wantonly, as he scooped her off her feet to lift her body and ground his hard length against her aching core.

"Fuck me," she demanded against his lips, her voice husky and breathless. She wanted, needed, was insatiable for his touch.

With feral eyes and surprising strength, he maneuvered their bodies, positioning himself at her entrance. Sliding her down, he impaled her on his hard shaft, and she gasped, followed by a loud, primal moan escaping her throat. He moved in and out of her with long deep thrusts, the sound of their wet skin colliding, echoing through the small space. With each powerful slide, he plunged impossibly deeper and made her cry out for more or to take her harder, her mind a chaotic mess of need and want. Everything about their connection was voracious and raw as he pummeled into her body again and again, bracing her against the hard tile wall. Juli could feel the sweet release building low in her belly as each punishing thrust and grind of his hips brought her higher.

"Come with me," he rasped out in a demanding growl.

With his command, she fell over the edge, letting the white-hot pleasure rip through her body like a tornado, a storm of sweet release. She could feel him swell inside her and let go, letting the storm carry him away too. Her spasming body milked every bit of pleasure from him till they were wrung out and spent. Their chests heaving, he anchored her against the shower wall, their foreheads meeting as the steam rose around them and they tried to catch their breaths.

"Are you okay?" he asked, meeting her lust drunk eyes.

"Yes." she managed as he slid out of her and set her gently on the tile floor. She wobbled, her knees weak from the pleasure, and he pulled her into his arms to ground her. Their eyes met, both not able to contain their grins as he said, "I don't have a frame of reference on this, but I believe that's what you call mind blowing shower sex."

She giggled, burying her face in his chest; she didn't have a frame of reference either. Most of what she knew she had done with Layne. A question lingered in her mind and hovered on her lips. *Should I ask?*

"Have you been with other women, after me?" she asked, the curiosity getting the better of her as she told herself it didn't matter what his answer was.

"I have dated. I have kissed a few women. But slept with any of them? No. You are still the only one."

She looked at him surprised, his answer not what she had expected, and questions started flying through her head. *He is in a rock band. He is handsome and wonderful. How did he not have other partners in the eight years they were apart?*

"Are you serious?" she asked, not quite sure what to say about this revelation. Although she was shocked, she felt overcome by this deep sense of honor that he had waited for her.

"Very serious, a lot of taking care of business myself," he said with a playful waggle of his eyebrows, then his face turned serious. "Whenever I kissed another woman, the desire wasn't there. It felt empty, no spark. They just weren't you."

Speechless and not sure what to say about his confession, she turned and adjusted the spray so they could wash themselves. She watched him, their eyes meeting as questions continued to float round and round her head. An endless barrage of questions.

After their shower, they crawled into her bed and she curled around him, resting her head on his chest with his arms wrapped around her securely. She lifted her head, resting her chin on her hand as she asked, "Why would you wait for me and not be with anyone else when you were the one that broke up with me?"

His lungs emptied with her question, and he stared at her a moment, then looked up at the ceiling. She could see his mind formulating how to respond to the question, needing to gather up the right words to say. He met her gaze as he responded. "First of all, I was wrong to have broken up with you, especially the way I did. It was immature, insensitive, and selfish. It is my biggest regret in life," he said, his eyes full of remorse. "I loved you very much, so much I'm not sure there are words to fully describe it. Even now, as I look at you, I can't come up with the perfect words to sum it up. I just do and I just know," he added, taking a deep breath, and letting it out slowly before he continued. "When you were gone, and I had pushed you out of my life, I went to a very dark place for a while. My parents noticed it, my band noticed it. Everyone was very concerned. I went through a lot of self-inflicted wallowing and loathing. I still loathe what I did to you. I'm still so ashamed of myself." His voice cracked with the admission, as he swallowed down hard. "As time passed, the feeling lingered but lessened. I went into a state of acceptance and tried to move on. But when I tried, no one could measure up. No one was you. The night we first slept together, I gave you my body, my heart, and my soul and when you went home, you took my heart and soul with you, and my body was left missing you."

She blinked at him, staring into his soft, sorrowful eyes. The eyes of the man she loved endlessly. Sighing, she rose over him to straddle his hips and she leaned down, kissing him softly and sensually. She had dated, but none to the point of intimacy. She knew now with his confession that their souls were connected in a deeply profound way and unknowingly she had waited for him too. She gazed down at him, feeling so much love for this wonderful man that she thought her heart may burst.

"There has only been you." She confessed, feeling tears rim her eyes.

His eyes reflected her emotion as she brought her lips to his, and she felt his arousal stir underneath her. She positioned herself and sank onto his length, sealing their bodies together. Body, mind, heart, and soul connecting. The look of pure love on his face and the exquisite feel of their coupling like a promise. A promise that they were meant to be together and somehow, someway, they would be.

CHAPTER 25

For four days, four glorious days, Layne lived in a state of insane bliss. In his mind, the universe had conspired and given them the reason, dare he say, the best reason to keep their relationship going, a baby. Their baby. Juli, the girl he loved hopelessly, was having his child and although they were too young and it was completely crazy, he, for one, was beyond excited. Juli, on the other hand, was in a complete state of panic, her texts to him full of fear and apprehension at the situation. As he read them and texted her back to reassure her, he was making plans, making decisions about their future. He would tell the band at his 18th birthday party in two weeks. Saying something like "Sorry guys, it has been a slice, but I got to split. Going to live in Hamburg, Germany with my pregnant girlfriend. You heard me right; I'm going to be a dad!"

He had thought about what he was going to say to his parents, something like, "These things just happen. Aren't you excited about having another grandchild on the way?"

Plus, they would visit, surely, they would visit. They loved Germany and would jump at the chance to visit their home country.

As for the fact that Juli still had two more years of high school to complete, he had that figured out, too. She would have the baby and he would stay home and care for their child while she went to school. When she got back from school, he would go to work, some retail job perhaps. Maybe a record store or music shop. They must have a lot of those in Hamburg. A job that would ensure he would be home at night to make love to her before they fell asleep wrapped up in each other's arms. Everything about his plan sounded perfect. They could do everything, be happy and have it all.

His phone dinged with what he assumed was another text from Juli. He opened their conversation, and in an instant, all his thoughts and plans for their future melted away with three little sentences.

Juli: I got my period. I am not pregnant. I am so relieved.

Layne fell back on his bed and covered his eyes with his arm, emotion rising quickly to the surface, as hot tears pricked his eyes, and spilled over, his last shred of hope to be with Juli and to live the magical life he had created in his head, blown away like dust by the warm summer wind.

* * *

It had been almost a week since she texted Layne that she wasn't pregnant and that all their worries were now over. She had been so relieved, chalking up her change in cycle to worry or stress about leaving Primrose and specifically leaving Layne. The thought of leaving this place and leaving him was literally painful. The ache in her heart was so excruciating, she cried involuntarily at night. *How am I going to say goodbye?* The word goodbye had so much finality, and she did not know if she could or would ever come back. She had fallen in love with Primrose in the time she was here. This community welcomed her in and made her feel like one of them. Everyone was so kind and sweet to her and although she knew Primrose wasn't perfect, it felt perfect to her.

Her mind drifted to Layne. Her sweet, thoughtful, loving boyfriend, who had given her so many firsts. *How am I going to wake up each morning knowing I would not be able to see him?* Layne had become her constant, her reason for waking up in the morning with a smile. Even before she would see him each day, she would get a text saying, "Good Morning, beautiful," and when they professed their love for each other a sweet "I love you.", would pop onto the screen. *Will he still do that when I am gone? Will he still send me sweet texts to let me know he is thinking of me?* She knew it wouldn't be the same with the change in time zone, but surely, he would try. She rolled herself out of bed and looked at her phone. No text from Layne. Something was bothering him; she could sense it. She was leaving in three weeks, and he was most certainly feeling the same way she was, wondering how it could all work. She needed to talk to him, to see him today, discuss those hard questions, and make some decisions to finalize their plan going forward. Juli fired off a text to him. At least with no pregnancy, they could make rational decisions, instead of impulsive ones.

* * *

IF WALLOWING COULD BE A SPORT, Layne would be an Olympian. For the past week, he did everything he could to shake off the doomsday feeling that was plaguing him. He spent his days moping around the house, deep in thought, not knowing what he should do, letting fear and doubt wrestle in his head. His 18th birthday was a week away, so he should be planning and thinking about all the fun they were going to have at his party. Instead, he was consumed by thoughts of his inevitable relationship demise with Juli. Any which way he looked at it. They weren't going to work after she left Primrose. They would have an entire ocean between them and couples even in different cities found it difficult, so how could they, at 18 and 16, make it work with so much distance between them? He knew he was overthinking everything, his chronic overthinking tendencies on overdrive. But now, with nothing permanently binding them together, he had no other choice. He had to break it off before they both got hurt.

He picked up his phone, seeing a text from Juli:

Juli: Can you pick me up today? I miss you and want to see you. I want to talk. Perhaps ice cream and we can go to our place or somewhere that we can be alone?

Alone with Juli. How was he going to be alone with her and utter those words that would break them both in two? His internal voices started to rationalize the situation. *She misses me now. After less than a week, how is she going to feel after months apart? I am doing her a favor, aren't I? Shielding her from the inevitable painful goodbye.* Knowing what needed to be done, he texted her back.

Layne: Yeah, I'll come get you. Be there soon.

Now if he could just muster the nerve to say what he needed to say to her. To tell her she means everything to him. That their time together had been the best time of his life, but he couldn't endure the next three weeks knowing they had no choice other than to end their relationship. Reaching for his keys, he made his way to the door, the weight of the end heavy on his shoulders.

JULI SAW Layne's car pull into the driveway and she skipped out the door, beyond excited to see him. Last time she saw him, there was so much fear and uncertainty with the possibility of a pregnancy and now it was just them again. No worries, just two kids in love wanting to savor every moment together before things changed. She opened the passenger door and slipped in, catching his gaze, her stomach sinking. Layne's eyes looked different, not as much sparkle as they always had when he saw her. Choosing to ignore his mood, she curled her hand around his bicep leaning towards him for a kiss as she said, "Hello, my strong boy."

Bridging the gap between them, she could feel Layne hesitantly give in, his body softening as she kissed him sweetly. She reached up and tangled her fingers in his hair, pulling away to meet his gaze before leaning in for another chaste kiss. He smiled reluctantly, a faint glimmer returning to his eyes. *There's my boyfriend.* She knew she had the ability to smooth out his edges, and she was ready to take advantage of that skill if she needed to.

* * *

THEY DROVE down to the Eazy, going inside to get soft serve cones and drove out of town a few miles to the utility road they liked to park on to make out. It had become their place to steal away and as of yet, they hadn't been caught. Layne glanced at Juli as they finished their ice creams, and she could see he had a lot on his mind. Grabbing a napkin, she dabbed her mouth and turned to face him. He rested his head on the headrest and turned to face her, his eyes turning flat and lifeless again.

"We need to talk," she started. "I go home in three weeks, and we need to decide how we are going to keep what we have going."

He didn't move, his eyes still locked on hers, not a hint of acknowledgement in their depths.

"I think we need to try to make this work. I know it will be hard, and we won't be able to see each other like we do now, but this..." she said, gesturing between the two of them. "...is too good to just end it when I go."

He still didn't budge, not even a flash in his eyes at her words. Only a blank stare.

"I love you, you love me, and that is enough for me. I know I will stay committed to you and I will try to see if I can come back next summer and perhaps you can come to me. I don't know. All I know is I want to try."

Finally, he lifted his head, but broke eye contact, choosing to stare out the window towards the wheat field next to them. He sat there saying nothing for a few minutes and Juli, who prided herself on always being happy and positive, started to feel anger and frustration envelop as each second passed. *Why is he not responding? Why is he just sitting there ignoring my words?* Desperate for him to respond and her annoyance with him growing by the minute, she reached over and gripped his bicep, something she knew he liked.

He turned, looked down at her hand on his arm and let out a long exhale, slowly meeting her frustrated gaze. But they were not the kind eyes of her sweet, loving boyfriend anymore. They were cold, resolute, and solemn.

"What do you think?" she tried. "Do you think we should try?" *He had to agree. He loved her, she loved him. A love like this does not come around every day. Yes, they were young, but love is love. He had to feel the same way.*

He opened his mouth and tried to say something, but then closed his mouth again.

Juli could feel her face get hot with frustration. *Why is he not responding? Why is he not talking?*

He turned away from her again, facing forward and started the car, putting it into drive and turning on the main road back to Primrose.

"Where are we going?" she asked in confusion, her eyes darting from him to the road in front of them.

"I'm taking you home," he said quietly, his voice quiet and monotone. "I don't think I can do this anymore, Juli."

What? What is he saying? He can not do this. What does he mean?

"What do you mean, Layne?" she asked, the pitch of her voice rising and her face flushing at his incredulous words.

He didn't answer, just turned towards Primrose, the town sign passing them, as he turned down her street.

"Are you going to talk to me? Did I do something wrong?" she reached for his bicep, gripping it tightly, her knuckles turning white, as he turned into Parker's driveway and parked the car.

He wouldn't make eye contact with her, and she became desperate for him to look at her. Give her something, anything. "Why are you doing this? What did I do?"

"You didn't do anything, but I think this is for the best. It was fun but I don't feel the same way you do," he said, his voice so flat and void of the sweet kindness she was accustomed to hearing from him.

She felt like she had been sucker punched. Her stomach roiled at his words as her face heated, flaming with incredulity. "Fun? It was fun. You don't love me?" she squeaked, blinking rapidly as tears spilled over onto her cheeks. "You told me you loved me. Were you lying to me?"

He didn't respond. He just sat there staring in the other direction, not looking her in the eye.

Betrayal filled her chest, anger, hurt, frustration, and overwhelming disappointment overflowing as she gritted her teeth and spewed words she never thought she would ever say to Layne. "You lied to me, strong boy. You said you loved me, you slept with me and now you do this. Are you breaking up with me?" she asked, disbelief making her nauseous. *How can I ask this question?*

He hesitated and let out another long exhale as he responded, sealing their fate, "Yes. It's for the best, Juli."

All color left her face with his final blow, her stomach curdling with nausea as bile rose in her throat. *He said he loved me, and he lied.* She had given him all of her, her body, mind and soul, and it wasn't enough. A hiccup escaped her throat, as she attempted to hold back a sob, the flood gates ready to burst. "I loved you." She whispered, reaching for the car handle. With one last glance at Layne, hoping against hope to see the boy she fell for, her heart shattered, because all she saw on his face was the end.

CHAPTER 26

Strolling hand in hand down the boardwalk of the Hamburg Hafen, Layne and Juli made their way down to the pier through the throngs of locals and tourists, weaving between vendors selling their wares. The Sunday morning Fischmarkt was an institution in Hamburg and Layne had never experienced anything quite like it. A man was shouting from his booth as he stood on a platform holding an eel, drawing curious spectators and customers. They strode over, taking in the scene and as they approached the booth, Juli asked, "Have you tasted eel before?"

"No, but I would try it," he replied as they each took a little sample from the vendor. Layne lifted the piece of meat to his nose and smelled it. It wasn't all that fishy a smell, so he popped it into his mouth and his eyes widened with approval. "It's good."

"Kind of sweet, right? Like lobster maybe." She compared.

He nodded and took her hand again as they strolled,

browsing with interest at all the beautiful things for sale. As they passed a vendor selling jewellery, Layne double backed, something in particular catching his eye. Immediately, his eyes locked on a silver ring, a delicate arrow making up the band. Memories of the necklace he gave her washed over him, and he smiled. Picking up the ring, he admired letting the morning light glint off the silver finish. Juli watched him curiously as he turned to her and asked, "Do you still have that arrow necklace I gave you?"

She frowned and replied, "Sadly, I do not. I used to wear it all the time, but then one day when I came home, it was gone. I think the chain broke, and it fell off, maybe on the U-Bahn. I do not know."

Reflecting her sadness about the loss of the keepsake, he looked at the beautiful ring again. So pretty. *Just like my girl.* Taking his wallet out, he handed cash to the vendor and turned to face Juli. She smiled as he took her hand and slipped the ring onto her ring finger, his eyes bursting with love and promise as he said, "Consider this an upgrade, and my promise to you we will always find our way to each other."

Her expressive eyes twinkled in the morning light as he smoothed his thumb over the delicate ring, looking so perfect on her hand. *Placing this ring on her finger feels like a promise of forever, but does it feel that way for her?* He was wrong before; he had made plans for their future, and she wasn't in the same place. He may have been young, but he knew what he wanted back then and what he wanted was her, no matter the circumstance.

Layne stared into Juli's eyes, hoping he was seeing what he thought was there, but fear and insecurity hovered on the edges as he considered the past damage he caused to her fragile heart. *Is that damage too deep or will the love we have for each other be enough?* With too many years of questioning his actions still plaguing him, before they could promise each other everything, she needed to know where his heart and head were eight years ago, just before it all came crashing down.

CHAPTER 27

EIGHT YEARS AGO

*I*f dying of a broken heart was indeed a thing, Layne was sure he was dying. He had spent the last week hulled up in his room, his concerned parents bringing him food as he tumbled deeper into the pit of despair he had dug himself into. He was turning 18 tomorrow, and he had cancelled his plans with his friends. He didn't want to see anyone. Just wallow alone in his dark, cold room. He deserved to be alone, after what he did to Juli. Everything he wanted to say refused to come out, instead leaving him unable to formulate the words and blurting out all the wrong things. His lack of explanation left him coming across as cold and mean, and she didn't deserve it. Every time he closed his eyes, he saw the desperation in her eyes when he started the car and turned towards Primrose. He could hear the crack in her voice as she pleaded for him to talk, to tell her what she did wrong. *How could she think she did something wrong? Juli was nothing but sweet, wonderful, and loving during our time together. She was perfect. Despite all of that, I broke her heart.*

He hung his head low as he gripped his hair and pulled tightly, needing to feel the pain rip into his scalp. Needing to feel even an ounce of the pain he had inflicted on her tender heart. He heard a commotion outside his room and his bedroom door flung open, smacking the wall, startling him. He looked up with surprise to see Harlow red faced and angry, flagged by Rex, Rami, and Steve. She had daggers in her eyes and if looks could kill, he would be dead for sure.

"You fucking idiot." Harlow started, her voice coming out like a growl. "What did you do to Juli?"

Rex put his arm around Harlow's waist before she came at Layne, and he added. "What my girl is trying to say is, why did you break up with her, man?"

"Yeah! You sleep with her, then a month later say, 'that was fun', and 'I don't love you'! Why would you tell her you love her if you don't? Just to get in her pants!" Harlow shouted.

"Is everything okay down there?" Layne's mother called from the stairwell, concern in her voice.

"Yes, Mrs. Stark. Everything is fine down here." Rami replied, giving Rex a look like he better calm Harlow down.

Rami walked over to the bed and sat down next to Layne. "What gives, man? You and Juli were good, more than good last I heard, and now you just ended it?"

"I thought you two were going to try the long-distance thing. Juli mentioned to me that she was going to come out next summer." Steve added, folding his arms over his chest and leaning against his dresser.

Layne lifted his head, his eyes red rimmed and puffy,

and his mouth was set in a grim line as he croaked out, "I messed up."

"You think?" Harlow glared with incredulity, Rex still holding her back.

"I was so scared to say goodbye, so I thought breaking it off now would prevent pain for both of us. Then when I tried to tell her that the words wouldn't come out right, my thoughts scrambled, and it was a mess. I miss her so much." He croaked out as he swallowed down painfully. "I was wrong, I was dead wrong and now Juli won't talk to me. I tried. I tried to text her, but she blocked me," he explained, his voice coming out rough and cracked as tears filled his eyes again.

"Have any of you heard from her?" Rami asked, looking around at their crew, his face etched with concern.

"I heard from her yesterday, but when I tried to message her, my message came back unsent." Harlow replied. "She may have blocked all of us."

"What did she say?" Rami asked.

Harlow pulled her phone out of her back pocket and swiped it open. "She said Layne broke up with me. He lied to me. He didn't love me, and it was just a fun time for him. There is nothing for me to stay for now. I am going home."

Layne jumped to his feet and stared at Harlow. "She said she's going home. When? Soon or in 2 weeks, like planned?"

"No idea." Harlow answered. "Honestly Layne, if you did to me what you did to her, I would want to bail right away. Everything about this place would remind me of you."

Layne took in her words, complete panic taking over as he grabbed his car keys off his desk and sprinted up the stairs. Slipping on his shoes, he ran out the door towards his car, his friends following him outside as Rami shouted. "Are you okay to drive?"

He didn't answer. There was no time to waste. He needed to get to Juli. He needed to apologize, to tell her he was an idiot and was wrong to say what he said. She was everything to him. Everything.

He peeled out of the driveway, kicking up dust as he went. The five-minute drive to town was like an eternity as he tried to formulate his apology. His plea to make it alright. He needed to get to Juli and to see her beautiful face. Pulling into Parker's driveway, he got out of his car and ran to the door, knocking loudly rather than ringing the doorbell. Mrs. Parker opened the door with a surprised look on her face.

"Layne." she said, obviously shocked to see him and likely even more shocked to see the panic in his sorrowful eyes.

"Is Juli here? I need to talk to her," he said, trying to get the words out all at once.

"Layne, she's not here. We took her to the airport yesterday. She went home," she said, with compassion in her voice.

Layne stumbled back, feeling the sting of her words repeating in his head. *She went home. She went home. She went home.* All the color drained from his face, and his chest tightened painfully as her words sank in. *Juli went home.*

"Are you okay Layne?" Mrs. Parker asked, her brows knitting together as she took in his stricken expression. "I'm so sorry that you missed her. I'm sure you can call or text her. I'm sure she would love to hear from you."

Layne nodded as Mrs. Parker hesitantly closed the door. He turned and took a seat on their front stoop, hanging his head in defeat. Hot tears painfully stung his eyes, but nothing would spill over. *You don't deserve the relief that tears would bring. You deserve to hurt like her.*

Time passed, dusk started to descend and still he sat, with no comprehension as to the hours that ticked by. A light turned on as the front door opened, illuminating the stoop where he sat. Mr. Parker strode out and took a seat beside him. He sat there quietly with him, in contemplative silence, as if giving himself or Layne a chance to formulate their thoughts. Finally, Mr. Parker spoke, his tone firm and resolute.

"Layne, you need to go home, son," he said. "You've been out here for four hours." Layne turned his gaze to him; his face anguished and his eyes glistening with unshed tears. "Your parents are worried about you and have called several times. You need to go home."

Layne got to his feet, his legs feeling numb and cold from the hard concrete stoup. Bracing himself against the house, a moment to adjust to standing, Mr. Parker rose too and put his hand on his shoulder, "You're going to be okay, Layne."

Layne met his compassionate gaze, and he could see

that he knew what Layne had done to Juli. Guilt and shame washed over him with that realization, making him turn his gaze away. Layne walked slowly to his car; shoulders slumped in defeat. It was officially over. *Juli is gone.*

CHAPTER 28

They boarded a ferry, bound for one of Juli's favorite places to escape, Blankenese. Known to be one of Hamburg's most affluent neighborhoods, Blankenese was on the edge of the Elbe River. With its steep hillside residences, quaint cafes, restaurants and interesting shops, this popular tourist spot was most beautiful in the spring and summer, but at this time of year they wouldn't have to elbow tourists to see the magnificent views.

As the ferry pulled out of port, Juli wrapped her fingers around Layne's bicep and rested her head on his shoulder. It felt so good to be with him, playing the happy, contented couple she always hoped they could be. Three days ago, she was ready to get her job done and walk away from him forever, giving him a taste of his own medicine after what he had done to her. Now, all she wanted was for him to stay and for them to be like this forever. The irony of the situation wasn't lost on her. Eight years ago, it was him that pleaded for her to stay in Primrose, and now it was her feeling desperate for him to stay in Hamburg. The reality was that it was impossible. He was still on tour with Prairie Sound, and they still had almost two months of touring left before they returned to Canada. *You could follow them.* That thought had popped in her mind, but she immediately vetoed it as she had a job, an apartment, and bills to pay. This was going to take some finessing, but she wasn't going to say goodbye to Layne again, at least not permanently. Somehow, someway, they would figure it out.

"This is one of your favorite places?" Layne asked as the neighborhood of Blankenase came into view. "It's beautiful."

"Yes, it has very old and historic houses and apartments. It's built right on the Elbe River and has streets and stairs that wind up the hill to take you to a beautiful lookout." She shared. "There is a restaurant on top we can eat at if you want."

"Sounds good," he said, looking out the window, watching them approach the pier. He turned back to her and reached over, lifting her chin to meet her eyes. "Thank you for taking me around your city. It has been truly wonderful." He leaned in and kissed her chastely, his soft lips feeling like heaven against hers.

How are you going to let him go tomorrow? Although she hated the way he ended their relationship years ago, she felt a better understanding now why he did what he did. Even though the way he did it was that of an inexperienced young man; she understood now that he did it because he loved her and wanted to protect them both. As bad as it was and as bad as it felt when they broke up, she was not oblivious to the fact that it would have been much worse if they had to say goodbye as she was about to leave. It would have broken them both. In a weird and twisted way Layne had done the kindest thing he could have done for her. Or at least had attempted to.

They disembarked the ferry and strode across the strip of beach into the little village. Juli always loved how Blankenese felt like its own little country and not like part of Hamburg. They strolled the streets, browsing in shops as they climbed the perpetual staircase to the top. Seeing Layne's curiosity and wonder at everything was a joy she hadn't expected. He was so inquisitive and asked so many questions. She had always known how smart he was and that he had a mind that worked overtime. It was fascinating to watch him now, a grown man, taking in things so familiar to her with such interest. When she met Layne, he was so quiet and introspective, choosing to keep most of his thoughts to himself, but now he carried a confidence that came with maturity and knowing who he was. She still saw glimmers of the boy she fell for, but mostly she saw the man. A man she was deeply in love with.

Reaching the summit, both of their faces red and rosy from the chill and exertion of the uphill hike, they found the restaurant and slipped inside. Being met with the warmth of shelter, a hostess greeted them, bringing them to a table with a view of the water. Placing their food and drink orders, they stared out at the water, words between them lingering heavily in the air.

Both turned at the same time, saying each other's

names simultaneously, resulting in a fit of laughter from them both.

"Ladies first." Layne gestured for her to go ahead.

Juli glanced down at her hands, her finger smoothing over the silver ring adorning her ring finger as she tried to formulate the best way to address the elephant in the room. His impending departure. She needed to share her deepest thoughts and fears, this perhaps being the only chance she would have to do it. "I don't want this to end." she began meeting his inquiring gaze. "I feel like there is a reason we were reunited. A reason why you are here with me now. What the reason is exactly, I don't know, but I feel like the universe is trying to tell us something and you are meant to be in my life again."

"I feel the same way. I just don't know what it will look like for us." he replied, being brutally honest. "I do know, my life feels more complete with you in it. My feelings for you have never changed, Juli. Looking at you now, they feel stronger. I love you, Juli. I love you very much."

"I love you too," she said, reaching for his hand and lacing her fingers with his, feeling tears prick her eyes as she let out a little giggle. "You know, a few days ago, I thought I would see you and feel hatred towards you. I had so much animosity built up inside of me towards you and I was just going to do my job, give you a piece of my mind and walk away, not looking back. But now, I don't think I can say goodbye. I don't think my heart could take it."

"We don't need to, Juli. I want to try to make this work long distance. I know it's not ideal and you have reasons to stay here, and I have my parents, my band who need me back in Primrose, but I will try to come back to see you as much as possible. Do you think it's possible for you to visit me?"

"I can try. I do have holidays sometimes." She replied, meeting his eyes. So much hope in her heart.

"Well, then that will have to be enough for now," he replied, tracing circles on her palm. "I will call you all the time and we can video chat too if it works for you. I'll call you in the middle of the night if I have to. A little lost sleep is worth it to see your face."

"It will not be easy, but I love you too much to not try, Layne." she said, a single tear escaping through her long lashes as she offered him a melancholy smile

He nodded and brought her hand to his lips, placing a tender kiss on it. "I love you, Juli. I never stopped loving you," he confessed, emotion rippling across his face like the waves outside cresting across the water. Layne looked out the window, taking in the view as he let out an exhale and his eyes drifted back to hers, another confession on his lips. "You know, I don't think I told you this, but I regretted how I broke things off with you immediately. The guys and Harlow, you remember her, right?" She nodded, smiling fondly at the memory of her dear Canadian friend. "They found out what I had done and ripped me up over it. I was already in a state of complete repugnance, and they let me have it. Harlow especially, she kept asking me, how could I do that to someone I love," he said, his voice breaking with his words. "You know, I came looking for you, wanting to apologize about a week later."

Juli's eyes grew wide as she asked, "You did?"

"I did. I felt so terrible about what I said, and how I

said it and since you blocked my texts, I drove to Parker's asking to speak to you," he said, intense sadness and regret reflecting in his eyes. "They told me you left early for home." She nodded, her face as pain stricken as his. "I sat on their front stoop for hours until Mr. Parker told me to go home."

"I didn't know that," she replied. "I wish I knew."

He gave her a half smile and shrugged, looking down at their intertwined hands. "I wish I had handled everything differently. Who knows, if I hadn't broken us up, maybe we could have made it work. Maybe we'd be married right now with a few kids or something."

Her heart was filled with regret, too. They had both made mistakes and perhaps if they had stuck it out, they wouldn't have lost so much time together. "Do you actually think of us that way in the future? Married with kids?"

"All the time," he confessed, his eyes locking on hers. "I know it's completely absurd, but I was so disappointed when you told me you weren't pregnant."

She leaned back in her chair, surprised by this confession as she replied, "I didn't know that."

"I know it's completely stupid, with us being so young, but you being pregnant was an excuse for me to do something impulsive, like move to Germany with you. It gave me as good a reason as any to say goodbye to my life in Primrose. Not that I wanted to say goodbye to my home, but my desire to be with you was greater than my obligations."

"So, you really would have given up everything for me?" she asked, incredulity in her question.

"In a heartbeat," he replied, meeting her questioning gaze.

Juli let go of his hand, sat back and reached for her wine, taking a sip, biding her time before she responded, turning her gaze to the view outside. A contemplative silence fell on the pair before Juli turned back to meet Layne's patient gaze, a hint of mirth sparkling in her eyes. "I am glad you did not have to make that choice. You would not be Layne Stark, bass guitarist for Prairie Sound touring with the Rolling Stones if you did."

Layne chuckled lightly, as his brows drew together, and his face turned serious. He leaned forward, his gaze meeting hers with an expression so loving and sweet it made her heart skip a beat. "You know none of that matters to me, right? I love what I do, but I love you more. I felt that way eight years ago and I still feel that way now."

This man. He was ready to sacrifice everything for her. Could she do the same for him? She glanced down at the ring on her finger. *An arrow. A symbol of direction. I could really use some direction right now.*

CHAPTER 29

PRESENT DAY

*L*ayne breathed in the sweet smell of Juli, wrapped up in his arms, fast asleep. After they returned from Blankenese they took the U-Bahn back to her apartment where they savored every last moment they could with each other. He made love to her, slow and tender, wanting to memorize her body, her face, her sounds, the exquisite feel of simply being with her. Everything about them together felt right. Felt perfect. And yet, it was far from perfect. They were in the same place they were before, wanting nothing more than to be together but having to live an ocean apart. This time was different, though. Their years apart had taught them one thing. That they were each other's soul mates. There could be a thousand oceans between them, and their souls would find each other every time.

His phone buzzed on the nightstand, and he glanced at the time. 5 a.m. Their time was almost done. He swiped open his phone, a text from Rami.

Rami: So sorry to do this to you, but our train leaves a little earlier than expected. We can come get you in the car. Send me your location and I will give it to the driver. Meet us on the street in a half hour.

Layne put down his phone and glanced down at Juli. Her long lashes fanned out on her cheeks, her plump pink lips positioned in a contented smile as she slept. "You are so beautiful, my sweet Juli." he whispered as he kissed her shoulder. She stirred, giving him an opportunity to slip out from under her, not wanting to wake her up. He quickly got dressed and looked around for a piece of paper and pen on her desk. Finding what he needed, he wrote her a note:

My beautiful Juli,

First of all, I need you to know; I love you so much. Through all this time, through all the distance, you are the only one I have loved and the only one I could ever love. The other half of my soul.

I had to meet my train earlier than expected and the guys are picking me up. I didn't have the heart to wake you. You're so beautiful when you sleep. Please don't think me not saying goodbye was the same as before, a fool running away scared. This thing between us doesn't require a "goodbye" because this isn't the end for us. I hope you understand.

These past few days with you have been beyond what I could have hoped for or dreamed. Your ability to love and forgive astounds me. I haven't even forgiven myself for what I did to you and yet; you let me in and opened your heart to me again. I am grateful for every moment we shared over these past few days and for every moment we will share in the future. And yes, Juli, you and I have a future. Our love story is not over yet. I will call and email you soon.

All my love forever,

Layne.

He placed the note on her laptop where he was sure she would find it and turned to lean down and kiss her gently on the cheek. She stirred, her eyes fluttering, but she didn't wake.

With suitcase in hand, he turned one last time to look at her, his heart not wanting to leave but his head knowing he had no choice. "I love you," he whispered, his words lingering in the darkness as he left her apartment, not knowing when he would see her again.

* * *

JOLTING OUT OF BED, Juli woke with a start, her alarm not having gone off. She picked up her phone, 7:28 a.m. She looked around the room in a panic. "Layne!" she called out as she climbed out of bed, noticing his suitcase was gone. She went to the living room area, glanced in the kitchen, and looked in the bathroom. *He's not here.* Before she overreacted, she returned to her room, looking for any sign of him, and noticed a note on her laptop. *Juli,* the top of it read in Layne's familiar scrawl. She stood there a moment staring at it, then spotting something dark, peeking out from under the overhang of her platform bed. She reached down to pick it up. It was Layne's t-shirt from yesterday. She held it to her nose, inhaling deeply, the musky scent of him making her feel instantly soothed. Slipping his t-shirt on, she took one more deep indulgent inhale as she sat down on the bed with his note.

"My beautiful Juli,

First of all, I need you to know; I love you so much. Through time, through all the distance, you are the only one I have loved and the only one I could ever love. The other half of my soul."

She smiled wistfully at his poetic words and read on his sweet promise to her. She held it to her chest and closed her eyes. *It is not a "goodbye. Their story is not over.* She repeated, letting them comfort her and remind her heart that it wasn't the end for them and this time it was different.

Her phone dinged with a text, and she swiped it open.

Layne: Our train just left Hamburg city limits. I miss you already. I'm sorry again that I had to leave so quickly. The last few days with you were everything to me. I love you so much Juli and I promise I will find a way to see you soon. Oh, and don't forget to send me the article. The guys are asking.

The article! I forgot all about the article! Deadline is 9 a.m. Juli noticed a missed call from Peter and groaned. She dialed his number, and he answered on the second ring, his tone firm and scolding, "Juli, where's my article?"

"I am working on it now," she said, taking a seat at her desk and opening her laptop. "I have all my notes organized; I just need to write it. When do you need it?"

"Yesterday, but I noticed you were busy," he said with a slight hint of amusement in his tone. "Perhaps a certain bass player distracted you." *Shit, shit, shit. Her social media, he was on her social media.* "Get it to me by 9 a.m. and it will get here just in time to review and go to print for the Tuesday issue."

"Got it Peter. I am on it."

"And Juli, this better be a good article. There is a lot riding on it for you," he reminded her.

She swallowed down, nervousness sinking in along with the weight of this opportunity. "It will be Peter. I promise you."

He hung up, and she opened a file, attaching her phone to upload the photos she took of the band. Then she opened her notebook and started typing. The words flew onto the screen with ease. Everything she wanted to say about Prairie Sound, their interviews, the insights, the inspiration. Prairie Sound, a true success story, and their readers were going to eat it up.

She typed out Layne's quote on what it was like to be on stage, feeling his words deep within her soul, *"When you fall in love, you feel your heartbeat wildly in your chest, you feel so acutely aware of your surroundings and the person you are with, and you feel like you can conquer the world. That's what performing feels like. Like you are in the perfect place, at the perfect time, with the people you want to be with. It's falling in love with your music every single night and feeling like nothing is more amazing than that moment together on stage."*

Everything about being with Layne over the past few days felt like this. Like she was in the perfect place and the perfect time, with the only person she wanted to be with. If she was being honest with herself, it had always been that way with Layne. The moment their eyes met; her soul imprinted on his.

She finished her article and sat back in her office chair with a look of pride on her face. The article was done, but it was just the beginning of their story. His words sank in as she clicked the send button and pushed away from her desk. She had a lot to figure out and some hard decisions to make. She smiled as she pulled the neck of his shirt to her nose and inhaled his masculine scent, making a promise to herself and to them. *I will find my direction. We will be together.*

* * *

Juli was a little late for work that morning, but picked up coffee for her and Peter to try to soften the blow. A blatant attempt to pardon her tardiness and late article submission. She hadn't heard back from Peter after she sent it, and she was sure she was in trouble with him. Juli hesitantly got off the elevator and waved to the receptionist as she always did. The receptionist gave her a wider smile than usual as her eyes followed her down the hall. *That's weird.* Her fellow co-workers looked up from their cubicles as she passed, wide smiles on their faces too. She was so distracted by their overly bright greeting and the attention they were giving her that she inadvertently passed Peter's office.

"Juli, can I talk to you?" Peter called out, and she back tracked still holding the two cups of coffee.

"Oh, hi, Peter, sorry I am late, I got you a Latte." she said, handing him a cup.

"That's nice of you. Thank you. Have a seat," he said, his face stoic as he gestured to the chair across from his desk. She took a seat, bracing herself for whatever onslaught and reprimand was coming her way. He turned away from his laptop to face her, apprehension surely in her eyes as he rose from his desk and rounded it. Peter reached for the latte, leaned against his desk and crossed his outstretched legs, casually taking a sip from his coffee. He looked down at her with his piercing blue eyes as he towered over her. Juli was thoroughly intimidated now and gulped down hard, trying to steady her jack hammering heart. "Juli…" he began slowly, drawing out what he was going to say. Juli braced herself, internally wincing. "… you wrote an outstanding article." Juli's eyes widened in surprise, not sure if she heard him correctly, her brain needing a moment to catch up. "Juli, it was fantastic! The way you immersed yourself in their world for the day. The questions you asked were relevant and powerful, and the pictures were the icing on the cake."

"Wow, thank you," she said, blinking rapidly, still stunned by his compliments. "It was a fun experience and Prairie Sound was amazing."

Peter set down his coffee cup and steepled his fingers, narrowing his eyes as he stared at her for an uncomfortably long time, making her wonder if she should take her compliments and go or stay put to see if he was done. He pursed his lips as he added. "Juli, I have a proposition for you. I have a new position opening for a Social Media Editor. We want to modernize this publication to more than just print. We need someone with a good eye on trends and excellent writing and interviewing skills. An initiative taker that can work under tight deadlines and can bring interesting and meaningful content to our audience." Juli couldn't believe her ears. That sounded fantastic for sure, but writing? Would she still be able to write? It was something she truly loved and could never give it up. As if reading her mind, he continued. "Most of what you would do is manage and edit our social media pages. However, we want you to continue to write as part of a featured article each week. Your knowledge of music is way beyond your years, and I would still like you to do articles on music, not just here in Germany, but world-wide. Perhaps doing LIVE interviews with singers and bands, then posting on social media for *Entertainment Weekly*."

"That sounds amazing, Peter," she replied, looking down at her hands. "But I am not sure I can take on a new role. I am considering leaving Hamburg."

"Let me guess. You are thinking of moving to Canada." he replied, a knowing smile curving his lips as his eyes twinkled. *Is he intuitive or psychic?* She questioned, not knowing exactly how to respond to his comment. "I know, I know, I am probably being presumptuous, but I think you are wanting to follow your bass player." He picked up a printout of her article. "Layne Stark, the guy you attended school with when you lived in Canada."

She stifled a giggle at the absurdity of how he was reading her mind, then asked. "How did you know what I was thinking?"

He tilted his laptop to face him and clicked a few times, then turned around the screen. A picture of Juli and Layne was on the screen. Juli was snuggled into his chest, his arms wrapped around her, smiles wide and hearts in their eyes. A selfie that was taken yesterday at Blankenese. Juli looked at Peter and down at her hand, touching the arrow ring on her finger. Layne's promise to her that he would find a way to be together. He had countless reasons why he couldn't move to her, and she had nothing other than her job and memories to hold her back from moving to be with him. She glanced at the photo on the screen, pure happiness and love filling her heart. Emotion rose in her chest as her eyes drifted to Peter's.

"That is not the look of just friends," he said with a knowing smile. "That's the look of two people in love."

She let out a long exhale, feeling tears of joy prick her eyes as she asked, "Am I able to do this job from Canada?"

"I don't see why not. You can do this job wherever you are in the world, even Primrose, Manitoba."

A giggle escaped her throat, a nervous and excited reaction to this incredible twist of fate. It seemed the universe was listening and working to bring her and Layne together. She blinked and swiped a tear that escaped down her cheek. "Thank you, Peter." she rasped. "I would very much like to take the job."

"Good," he said, clasping his hands together. "Juli, I had been considering you for the job for a while, but this article you wrote..." he started pointing to the paper on his desk. "...this article is inspiring and very well written; it sealed the deal."

Juli blinked rapidly, more tears streaming down her face as emotion overtook her and she got up from the seat. Peter smiled, kindness painted on his face as he watched her swipe at her fallen tears. Although Juli was sure it wasn't appropriate, she bridged the gap between them and wrapped him in a hug, giving him a tight squeeze. He patted her back awkwardly and threw his head back in a big, bountiful laugh. "It's going to take a week or two to replace your other job and I assume you will have some logistics to figure out with your move, so if you need any days off, please let me know."

"I will." She replied, releasing her hold on him, grabbing her things, and heading towards the door.

"And Juli..." Peter added just as she was about to exit his office. She turned around, meeting his steely gaze. "...I am truly happy for you."

Juli beamed through her joyful tears and returned to her cubicle, her colleagues surrounding her with congratulations. All the pieces were fitting into place and the decision was officially made. She was going to leave Hamburg and be with the man she loved.

CHAPTER 30

With the fortunate chain of events, Juli had so much to do before she left Germany. Subletting her apartment, visiting her dad in the Netherlands, not to mention packing all her most valuable possessions and figuring out how she was going to get everything to Canada. *Could she get it all done on time?* Feeling nauseous at the thought of what she all had to do, she sipped her ginger tea as she sat bundled up on her little balcony, dreaming of her permanent reunion with Layne and the feel of his warm arms around her again.

First things first. She needed to talk to Mr. Parker. Over the years, she had kept in touch with her exchange family, and in the year she lived with them, she knew Mr. Parker did some immigration law.

Juli glanced at her watch and entered her kitchen, setting her mug on the counter as she strode to her bedroom and took a seat at her desk. It was early in the morning in Hamburg, but she made sure she was up early to make her appointment. With her laptop already queued, she clicked the link sent to her and within seconds, Mr. Parker's familiar face popped up on screen.

"Hello Juli!" he said in greeting. "It's so nice to see you!"

"Nice to see you too, Mr. Parker. I am excited to talk to you today!"

"I'm excited as well, Juli. From your email, you indicated you want to know how you can immigrate to Canada."

"Yes, that's correct." She confirmed with a smile. "I need to know what kind of process I am looking at and what the timeline would be."

"Before I go through that, I have to ask, does this have anything to do with Layne Stark?"

She glanced away and let out a little giggle, followed by a sigh as she replied, "It does. I want to move to be with him."

"I thought so," he said with a knowing smile. "That young man has held a torch for you, for years. He has become quite the success too."

She nodded and explained, "Layne and his band were here on tour a few weeks ago and we reconnected." She replied. "We love each other very much."

Mr. Parker shook his head and smiled wistfully. "I could always tell you did." He looked down at a paper on his desk and clapped his hands together. "Well then, let's see what we can do to get you here permanently and reunite you two love birds indefinitely. There is something we can do that would help your application to process quickly, which is family sponsorship. Basically, a Canadian resident would sign a Sponsorship Agreement stating that they will support you financially if you cannot support yourself. At a minimum, that type of agreement would take 10 months to process and up to 2 years."

"That is a long time." Juli said, her stomach sinking in disappointment.

"It is, but we can have you apply for a visitor's visa in the meantime, and you could be here in a few weeks if it goes through. You will need your passport up to date, you need to pay the fees for the visa which is around $500 Canadian, you need to get a criminal record check or the equivalent in Germany, you need to have a full medical exam and have a clean bill of health, there are some photographs you need to provide which I can send you the guidelines on and you need a letter from your employer that you have a means of income during your stay."

"I just accepted a new Social Media Editor position that will allow me to work anywhere in the world, so income is no problem." She replied.

"Good, good!" he replied. "The last thing you will need is a Proof of Ties letter to Canada, which I can write up for you. Also, if you would let me, we would like to personally sponsor your immigration."

Juli brought her hand to her heart. The Parkers had always been like family to her and, while she was there, treated her like a daughter. They had also been so kind to her when her mother passed away. To her, they were a second family.

"Thank you. I appreciate you so much." She said, feeling the emotion rise in her chest. "How long can I stay on a visitor's visa?"

"Six months, but we could get it extended. Also, if Layne decides he wants to marry you, we could have you apply for immigration under Spousal Sponsorship. Is that a possibility?"

Juli had to think about that for a moment. He had confessed to her he had thought about them getting married before, and the thought of marriage with him made her heart skip a beat. But was he thinking down the road, or was he ready to commit now, with a timeline so she could immigrate?

"Not sure," she replied honestly. "We have talked about the future and wanting it to be together, but marriage and future plans have not been discussed. Layne actually has no idea I am doing this."

"Do you plan on telling him?" Mr. Parker asked.

"I was hoping to surprise him." She replied.

"Well, then let's get everything you need together for the Visitor Visa and once you're here, we can see where you and Layne are at. Either way, you are coming to Canada, Juli, and I am so happy to help you."

Juli ended their call, bursting with excitement as she sat back in her office chair, and picked up the list she wrote down on what she needed for the Visa. It was a lot, but she was up for the challenge. She pulled up the offer letter from *Entertainment Weekly* for her new job and printed it off. That was proof of employment – check. She reached into the drawer in her desk and pulled out her passport. Five more years left, good, that was done - check. An email popped up from Mr. Parker with a link to pay the Visa fees, so she grabbed her credit card and went ahead and paid them – another check. Then she perused what she still needed. Medical, criminal record check, photographs, and letter of ties to Canada.

She looked at the time on her computer. Her doctor's office would be open in 20 minutes so she could make an appointment. Her stomach roiled. She felt hungry and nauseous. So much to do, so little time. Perhaps some toast and another ginger tea would go down nicely to relieve this feeling of being overwhelmed. She had a lot to do and only six weeks to make it all happen before Layne returned home to Primrose.

THE EUROPEAN TOUR was incredible and with each magnificent city, Layne wished Juli was there experiencing it with him. Although the tour was amazing, Layne had to admit, he was ready to go home. Part of him still lingered on the idea that maybe he should stay in Europe for a while, spend more time with Juli, but he had commitments waiting for him back home in Primrose. Besides, as wonderful as Europe was, three months away from Primrose was far too long. It was now late November, and he craved sitting out on his back deck, breathing in the cold crisp, fresh air. As nice as cities were to visit, he loved the country more.

God, I miss Juli. They had emailed, texted and even video chatted, although he knew video chatting would likely be hard once he got home with the time difference. Yet, he was still going to try. He needed to see her, know she was still in this with him, and to hear her beautiful, melodic voice. One positive thing that came out of their being apart was that he had notebooks full of lyrics for their second album. Juli, coming back into his life, became a source of inspiration and she was his muse. Gone were the sad, sorrowful songs about the one that got away, replaced by songs about true love.

Seeing the town sign for Primrose come into view, he sighed. Savannah glanced behind her and gave him a knowing smile. "Happy to be home?" she asked. Rami glanced at him in the rearview mirror.

"Yeah, it's funny. You can travel all over the world and see so many incredible cities, but coming back to this quiet town always feels like you're being wrapped up in a hug."

"I think that's a sign that you are exactly where you belong." Rami added, meeting his eyes in the mirror and glancing over to Savanah, reaching for her hand. "It helps when you have someone at home waiting for you, too."

Layne wanted that so much. He wanted that with Juli. Last they spoke on video, Juli shared that she was starting as a new position for *Entertainment Weekly*. Her article about Prairie Sound acted as a catalyst for the promotion. He had read the article, which captured him and his band-mates perfectly and was so proud of her. The only thing that worried him was that maybe this job meant that they would never live in the same place. With *Entertainment Weekly* being a German publication and their office in Hamburg, a promotion grounded her like an anchor to her home city, just like his band and family grounded him to Primrose.

"Rami told me you reunited with her high school girl-friend while on tour." Savanah said as they turned down his road. "I saw your social media pictures. She's very beautiful, Layne. What's her name again?"

"Juliana or Juli." he replied. Just saying her name made pangs of longing start again. He needed to call her when he got home. She would likely be sleeping, but hopefully she would pick up. He needed to hear her voice and perhaps it would tie him over till their next video call.

It was dark, after 9 p.m. and the yard light turned on as they drove onto the driveway. Layne glanced at the house and could make out the silhouette of a figure on his front porch, but it was too dark to make out who it was. *Perhaps Mom and Dad are here welcoming me home*. He squinted as they pulled up next to the garage and parked.

Rami and Savanah got out of the car, and Layne protested. "It's okay, guys, I got my bags, seriously you probably want to get home," he said, his brows drawn together as he pulled his suitcases out of the trunk of the car. "Seriously, I got this."

Rami and Savanah simply smiled and looked toward the house, his eyes following their gaze. Squinting through the darkness, he tried to make out the person standing in the dim light of his porch that captured their attention. A beautiful woman stood there, tall, dark hair, large doe-like eyes. A woman that looked like Juli. Unable to process what he was seeing, he closed his eyes and opened them again, sure it was just a manifestation of his earlier thoughts. The woman descended the stairs and strode down the walkway, now bathed in the yard light. Layne shook his head, not believing his eyes as he dropped his suitcases and started walking towards her, picking up speed, his legs not going quick enough. She ran to him too and jumped into his arms, curling her legs around his waist. He inhaled deeply her spicy vanilla scent and hot, disbelieving tears pricked at his eyes. *It's her. Juli is here!* He pulled his head back, looking into her expressive brown eyes, those beautiful eyes he saw every time he fell asleep at night. They glistened in the yard light, brimming with happy tears. He captured her lips, as he kissed her long and hard, before his lips trailed over her beautiful face, making her giggle with his onslaught of kisses. Releasing their embrace, he set her on her feet and gripped her face in his hands, needing to simply look at her to know this was real and not a dream.

"What are you doing here? How did you get here?" he asked, his eyes searching hers. Too many questions wanting to tumble out all at once.

"I have been here for a week, staying with the Parkers." she replied. "I connected with Rami, and he put me through to Savanah so her and I have met and have been messaging each other all day."

Rami and Savanah walked up, both giving Juli a hug in greeting.

"How long are you here for? Please tell me I have more than a few days with you," he said, pulling her into him.

She looked up through her long lashes, meeting his eyes again, a sweet smile tugging at her lips. "I am here indefinitely if you will have me. I have started the process of immigrating to Canada."

Layne's eyes widened as tears pooled and overflowed onto his cheeks. "You're moving here for me? What about your new job?

"My new job is mobile and..." Juli smiled and reached

for his hand, placing it on her belly, "I am moving here for us."

His eyes widened and flitted to his hand on her stomach, then back to her eyes, surprise, shock, every possible emotion crashing together as he asked, "Are you pregnant?"

She nodded, blinking rapidly as tears trailed down her cheeks. *A baby. Our baby.* Layne fell to his knees in front of her, right there on the snowy driveway, and kissed her belly tenderly. He looked up, meeting the eyes of the woman he loved more than life itself, the only woman he would or could ever love as he asked, "Juli, will you marry me?"

Juli blinked in surprise, and swiped at the wetness on her cheeks, her lips curving up into a wide smile as she answered, "Yes, Layne, I want nothing more."

He rose to his feet and swept her into his arms, swinging her around. She threw her head back and giggled, the sweet melodic laugh that made his heart sing. He set her on her feet and touched her stomach again. "I love you both so much."

Rami cleared his throat, breaking their revery. "I think Savanah and I need to leave you two alone." Rami said, taking Savanah's hand, who was wiping tears from her face now too. "Let's go beautiful," he said, pulling Savanah into him and kissing her on the head. He glanced back at Layne and offered him a knowing smile.

Layne swept Juli into his arms, making her squeal as he trudged down the snowy walkway towards the house. "Your luggage." She giggled.

He glanced at his suitcases sitting in the middle of the yard and shrugged. "I'll get them later."

She threw her head back with laughter as he carried her to the front door and fumbled in his pocket for his house keys. Finding them, he unlocked the door, opened it, and looked deep into Juli's beautiful brown eyes. "Welcome home," he whispered, emotion straining his words as he stepped over the threshold of their new life together.

ONCE THE WORD got out that Juli was moving to Primrose, the gossip mill was having a field day. They were the talk of the town and Layne's phone, and email was full of messages from friends and family so excited about their engagement. His parents were beside themselves with excitement about their impending marriage and were beyond thrilled about their new grandchild on the way. Once the excitement died down, and with Layne on a much-needed hiatus from performing, there was nothing left to do but get completely lost in each other.

They lay in his bed, tangled up in the sheet, both satiated and happy. Juli curled her naked body around Layne, resting her head on his chest, feeling the steady thrum of his heart against her cheek. She sighed, reaching up to run her fingers through the rough stubble forming on his face. They hadn't left this bed, for she wasn't sure how many days, eating, sleeping, making love, completely encased in a warm love bubble. "Will we ever get out of this bed?" she asked, making languid circles on his bare chest.

"Not if I can help it," he replied with a contented grin. "Now that I have you, I can't get enough of you."

"Passion was never our problem," she replied, climbing on top of him, straddling his hips. He trailed his hands down her sides, watching the goosebumps form on her creamy skin. His hand rested on her belly as he caressed where there would soon be a bump.

"You are going to be so beautiful pregnant." He said, his gaze drifting from her stomach to meet her eyes. "I feel like things happened the way they were supposed to happen. You, here with me carrying our child. I can't wait to marry you."

Juli leaned forward, capturing his lips in a long languid, sensual kiss before she answered. "I would marry tomorrow if we could. You know, I don't want or need a big wedding. I just need you and me and maybe a few friends and family." He laced his fingers with hers as he thought about her request. He didn't need anything elaborate either. All he wanted was to make her his wife.

"How about February 14th, the day of love?" he said, wagging his eyebrows.

She let out a little giggle at this as she replied, "Isn't every day for us a day of love?"

"True, but seriously, it gives us almost two months to plan a wedding, maybe get your dad and stepmom to fly out, perhaps your brother too," he said, selling her on the idea. "Savanah is an event planner, and she can plan everything for us. We would just need to show up and say 'I do.'"

"That sounds good to me," she said, holding out her hand that had the arrow ring on it.

"What kind of engagement ring do you want?" he asked, watching her.

"I don't need one." She said, putting her hand close to her heart. "This ring is perfect."

"God, I love you," he declared as he flipped her onto her back and settled between her legs, his strong arms caging her to the mattress.

She took his face in her hands. "There is nowhere else I would rather be. I love you, strong man. Always have, always will."

He kissed her tenderly, their bodies joining in sweet union. Two crazy kids in love and finally going the same direction.

EPILOGUE

5 YEARS LATER IN SUMMER

Layne glanced out the kitchen window, watching Juli and their 4-year-old daughter Tabitha exit their garden and walk across the backyard. Juli had her long dark brown hair pulled up in a messy bun and their daughter had hers pulled back the same way. She was Juli's mini-me, a spitting image of her beautiful mother. Juli held Tabitha's hand, clutching the sling on her chest, holding their six-week-old son, Sebastien. He watched as she laughed, throwing her head back. Their smart and sassy daughter likely telling her one of her silly stories. Tabitha was just as bold and fearless as her mother, and Layne already knew he was going to have to keep a close eye on her, especially when she was old enough to take an interest in the boys. She was going to be a handful; of that, he was certain.

God, I love her. His eyes drifted back to Juli and the wonderful years they had spent together since their reunion. He thought back to their wedding, a small affair, held at a quaint bed-and-breakfast on the edge of town.

Only those most important to them in attendance. It was understated, intimate, and perfect for them. He could still see his beautiful Juli walking towards him down the aisle, radiant in white chiffon, her glorious baby bump on full display with red roses in her hair. The woman of his dreams.

He heard the screen door slide open as Tabitha's melodic giggle broke him from his reflection. "Hi, Papa." she said happily, her big brown doe-like eyes twinkling. "We were in the garden. She held up a bouquet of flowers to show him. "Mama says we can use these to make flower crowns so we can be fairy princesses at my party."

He crouched down, meeting Tabitha's expressive eyes and smiled, "That sounds beautiful, Tabs. Are you excited to be five years old tomorrow?"

"I am so excited." Tabitha replied as she handed Juli the bouquet and stepped into his arms. He swooped her up, Tabitha squealing with glee as he tickled her rosy cheeks with his facial scruff.

Juli rounded them as she set the flowers on the counter and leaned against it clutching the sling as she watched them, her eyes dancing with delight. Setting Tabitha down, he turned to Juli and sauntered over, caging her against the counter. His lips just a breath away from hers, he licked his lips and gave her his sexiest look as he said, "Hey there, hot momma."

"Hey there, strong man." She replied, running her hands up his arms, along his shoulders and threading her fingers through his hair, giving it a tug. He groaned, low and deep, as their lips met in a delicious kiss. Pulling her head back, she flashed him a look of approval as she raked her fingers through his growing beard, her eyes twinkling playfully. "You can use that scruff on me later." She whispered against the shell of his ear. "The Doctor gave me the green light."

A low growl rumbled from deep in the chest, knowing he was going to make love to his wife tonight. A sexy smile curled on Juli's lips as she leaned in to kiss him again, but just as their lips were about to touch, a little whimper and coo sounded from inside the sling, interrupting their embrace. Simultaneously, they looked down to see their son was awake and looking up at them with his sweet brown eyes.

"Seb, we're going to have to discuss timing." Layne said with a laugh.

Juli, mirroring his laughter with her signature giggle, asked, "Can you take him for a while so I can trim these flowers?"

"Of course," he replied, helping her unravel the sling. Juli handed him the baby, and he reached for a blanket, cradling their tiny son in his arms. It was a beautiful summer day, so he stepped outside onto the deck, taking a seat in the shade of the awning, and looked down at his son, happy and content in his arms. Sebastien gripped his finger and emotion rose to the surface, so much love bursting from his heart. Smiling, he looked deep into his son's eyes as he said, "Hello, my sweet boy." Sebastien gurgled in response, his lips turning up in a smile. Layne chuckled. *Probably gas, but I'll take it.* "I think it's time you and I have a man-to-man talk. I got to do this early, so you don't make the mistakes I made, okay?" his son blinked in response. "I have three pieces of important advice for you that you need to remember." Sebastien yawned, but his eyes were still fixed on Layne's. "Number one, pursue your dreams with everything you've got. If you want to be a musician, like your papa, go for it. If you want to become a world class surgeon, go for it. If you want to be the president of Timbuktu, go for it." Sebastien blinked. "Whatever you want to do, know your mom and I will be cheering you on," he said, tracing his fingertips across Sebastien's delicate brows affectionately. "Number two, always be yourself. Even if you are not the most popular, or the handsomest, although if you end up looking like your mom, you are going to be a looker." Sebastien cooed in response, making Layne grin. "Even if you are kind of weird or a loner and most people don't quite understand you, know you will find friends that truly get you. And those friends will become family to you." Layne felt his words to his son deeply, thinking of his bandmates and how they met as awkward teenagers. His pseudo family. "And lastly, if one day a girl approaches you who is beautiful and has a smile that makes your heart skip a beat, offer her the seat next to you. You never know if that girl is the one and only girl meant for you. And if she is the one, hold on to her, and don't let her go. Don't let her get away." Sebastien started to fuss, and Layne lifted him onto his shoulder, cradling his head and bouncing him as he rubbed his back. "I know Son, you would never make that mistake, would you?"

"That was sweet." Juli said, standing by the patio door with two glasses of iced tea in her hands.

Layne shrugged; his eyes locked on his beautiful wife. "I got to impart my wisdom on my son."

Juli smiled brightly, her face beaming as she sauntered over and took a seat next to them.

He reached for her hand and brought it to his lips, kissing her arrow ring tenderly. It took them eight years to come back to each other, both needing to find their direction in life so that they were ready to be together again. Every time Layne thought back on their story, even through all those years of doubt, thinking that he would never see Juli again, the universe was working its magic to bring them back together, two souls bridging the distance.

The patio door slid open, Tabitha's happy face greeting them as she climbed onto Juli to curl up in her lap. He looked down at his infant son, now sleeping peacefully on his chest, over to his beautiful daughter, her smile brighter than the summer sun, and up to Juli's gorgeous brown eyes. A lifetime of love in their depths. *Thank you, universe.*

Continue reading about the members of Prairie Sound in the next book, ***Love Notes.*** Buy now!

ALSO BY TANYA RENEE

Primrose Series

Prairie Sky

Prairie Nights

Prairie Fire

Prairie Hearts

Prairie Sound

Prairie Rain

With The Band

Finding Direction

Love Notes

The Spring of Love Series

By Virginia Taylor

Forever Delighted

Forever Amused

Forever Heartfelt

The Tooth Fairy Chronicles

By Victoria Rocus

Tooth Decay With A Side Of Fae

Toothaches And Wedding Cakes

Baby Tooth And Tangled Roots

Wisdom Tooth And The Awful Truth

A New Page

by Aimee MacRae

It Happened in Paris

By Michelle Beesley

The Bondi Bubble

By Megan Krolik

For more information visit:

www.serenadepublishing.com

ABOUT THE AUTHOR

Tanya Renee is a proud Canadian Prairie girl, who grew up on a family farm in Southeastern Manitoba Canada. Always an avid reader, she became intrigued with the romance genre at an early age when she first read Romeo and Juliet. Soon after she started to craft her own stories and poetry and by the time she was in high school, she had declared someday she would become a writer.

Married to the love of her life, she resides in Steinbach, Manitoba Canada with two teenagers and a menagerie of pets. When she's not cooking up a storm in her kitchen, she can be found tinkering in her garden, drinking copious amounts of coffee with a book in hand, listening to 80's music/audio books or at her laptop creating stories that are emotionally satisfying. She writes what she wants to read, epic stories that bring you on a journey and make you believe in love.

www.tanyareneeromance.com

ACKNOWLEDGMENTS

I would like to thank my readers for your loyalty and dedication. Every message, every review, every comment is read and appreciated. Your kindness, enthusiasm and excitement to read my stories has made this journey so sweet! Thank you for being my co-pilot on this exhilarating ride. I love you all!

To my exchange partner and friend, Alice Kraft who inspired this story. The year we spent together, half in Canada and half in Germany changed my life forever. Thank you for all the laughter, the fun, and what you did, to help a shy small town Canadian girl break out of her shell to be more confident and independent. I will always be grateful for you and the experience we shared.

To the beautiful city of Hamburg, Germany. A place rich in history, culture and charm. You will always have a piece of my heart.

To my parents, who said yes when I uncharacteristically came home asking to be part of an overseas student exchange. You gave me a gift by saying yes. Thank you for always doing your best for me and my siblings. I love you both.

To my husband, Bart, the grumpy to my sunshine. Your unfailing belief in me is why I continue to write. Thank you for your support and love.

To my son, Theo who is on the cusp of finding his direction, in the words of Dr. Seuss, *"You have brains in your head. You have feet in your shoes. You can steer yourself any direction you choose."* As your mom, I can't wait to see what your future has in store. Love you T!

To my daughter, Raina, who teaches me about empathy, authenticity and kindness every day. I could not be prouder to be your mom. Love you!

And lastly to Sarah Williams, fellow romance author and CEO of Serenade Publishing. Thank you for all the commitment and hard work you put into my books as well as the other Serenade authors. I am truly grateful to consider you not only a mentor but a friend.

www.ingramcontent.com/pod-product-compliance
Lightning Source LLC
Chambersburg PA
CBHW060554190726
48283CB00003B/1007